FIRE OF THE WOLF

The Gray Pack #1

LORI KING

BLURB

After a devastating fire, Caroline Trainor is left homeless and feeling hopeless. Her entire life is gone, but to her surprise, she's far from alone.

Devin and Damon Gray have spent their entire lives leading their Wolf Pack as well as their Firehouse. They know how to manage people, but managing a mate is an entirely different subject.

From moment one, Caroline feels a connection to the twins, but she doesn't want to lose her own identity. Struggling with unresolved pain from her past, she has no desire to become their house-wolf—until another wolf pack's alpha threatens their lives and relationship.

For my Mom who has read countless pieces that I have written over the years and continued to encourage me to reach for my dreams.

For my Dad who has always been my rock of stability, and the hand that picks me up when I fall.

For my Sister who is my rough draft editor, best friend, and fellow romantic.

For my Brother who keeps me laughing and reminds me that success isn't always tangible.

For my Husband who is my knight in shining armor. You will always be my favorite hero.

And for my children who remind me that life is short, and you must grab it with both hands.

I hope to always Live, Laugh, and Love like today is my only chance.

Always~Lori

CHAPTER ONE

Sweat trickled down her brow and into her eyes as Caroline belly crawled down the hallway as fast as her burning lungs would allow. The acrid smell of smoke made her nose run, as stinging tears spilled down her cheeks. Molly and Tyler were in the apartment down the hall from hers, and she had to get to them, had to help them. Giving up was not an option.

Minutes before, when the smoke alarm in her apartment went off, Caroline nearly jumped out of her skin. She couldn't smell the smoke until she opened her apartment door and found the hallway outside filled with a thick black fog of it. Her mind flashed immediately to a smiling Tyler, who had been playing in the hallway just a couple of hours ago with a baseball and glove, waiting for her to come home from work so that he could show her that he lost another tooth. She had laughed and hugged him while she walked him to his apartment door, and waved a quick hello to his mom, Molly. Molly had invited her into the apartment for dinner, but after a twelve-hour shift at the hospital, Caroline just craved quiet.

Unloading her work bag, purse, and jacket just inside her apartment door, she'd stripped her clothes off for a hot shower, only stopping on the way to snag a bottle of wine and a glass from her tiny kitchen. After scalding away the tension in her muscles, and downing a full glass of wine, she slipped on her comfiest yoga pants and settled onto the couch to watch her favorite Thursday-night TV programs.

Roughly sixty minutes later as she crawled for all she was worth, all she could think about was Tyler and Molly trapped in their apartment and scared, or worse. She could barely focus with the screaming sound of the fire alarms in the apartment building's hallway, but her gut told her that Molly wouldn't have chanced the thick smoke, and would have directed Tyler to the windows of the apartment to scream for help instead. Caroline knew that they had to get out of this building as fast as possible. Having been built in the early 1960s, the building was barely livable, and wouldn't survive a fire that produced this much heavy smoke. When the structure came down, she was determined that she would be safely out with Molly and Tyler.

As she pushed open their apartment door, she gasped in the fresher air, and heard Molly screaming for help to her left. She was able to get up to her knees and call back to them.

"Tyler? Molly? We have to get out of the building, come to the door, and I'll help you out! Hurry!"

"I'm scared, Caro!" Tyler's voice came out raspy, and his breathing was wheezy, but she was able to see him about ten feet from her, curled up on the floor with Molly's arms around him.

"No, Caroline! The fire department will come and get us. We can't take Tyler through the smoke. Shut the door to keep it out of here." Molly was in pure panic mode.

Caroline groaned in frustration. She understood Molly's fears. Tyler had asthma and had to take daily breathing treatments to keep from having asthma attacks. Smoke like this was especially dangerous for him, but Caroline knew she was right about this situation.

"Molly, the fire department won't get here in time. Tyler pull your flannel shirt off and tie it around your face like a cowboy's bandana. That will help you keep the smoke out, and when we get outside, we

2

will get you some medicine. Molly grab a towel or something to cover your face, now. We are leaving this building together, right now."

Caroline began herding the two out the apartment door when she heard the first creak and groan of the building. Her heart leapt into her chest, and she tensed all her muscles, bracing for the impact that she was sure was coming, but the ceiling stayed above her, and the floor held beneath her, so she put her hand on Molly's butt and gave her a firm push out the door of the apartment.

"Hurry up!" she screamed as loudly as her raw lungs could take.

They all began moving down the hallway, crawling along on their hands and knees, because the only breathable air was next to the floor. The smoke was growing thicker and for the first time, Caroline began to doubt her ability to get them all out of there alive. She could feel the rough fibers of the commercial-grade carpet rubbing her elbows and legs raw. There was heat now, but she still couldn't see flames. Despite the high temperature, Caroline's skin crawled with goose bumps at the thought of a death by fire. Another surge of energy burst through her, and she pulled up alongside her two charges, urging them to move faster. She could hear Tyler's gasping breaths, and the fear that rolled off of Molly was almost tangible.

They made it down the first half of the stairs to the landing, and the air cleared slightly. Caroline could see the late evening sunlight at the bottom of the second set of steps filling the foyer of the building. She knew that help had to be just outside the glass doors. Suddenly, Tyler collapsed in front of her. She watched in horror as Molly stopped next to her son, coughing and choking on the poisonous air. She looked at Caroline and seemed unsure what she should do. Following her instincts, Caroline reached for her, and with a hard shove she pushed Molly down the last several steps, so that she wouldn't have to decide. Somehow Caroline managed to lift Tyler's body into her arms, and tumble the last few steps herself, holding him as close to her as she could.

She lay there with Tyler on top of her, staring bleary-eyed at the ceiling or what would have been the ceiling if she could have seen through the waves of dark smoke. Just as her world stopped spinning, she felt strong hands grasp Tyler, and pull him from her, while another set of hands held her under her arms, and quickly pulled her from the floor up against a huge muscular chest. Unbelievably, she could smell him through his fireman's suit, and the smoke. Her heart flipped over, and her head spun.

His arms gripped her tighter, and she smiled to herself, thinking, *Wow, isn't he a fantasy waiting to happen?* And then she passed out.

Shit. Damon looked down at the scrap of a woman he held in his arms. She'd just gone completely limp, and any second this building was coming down. He had to move fast. The other two people had been taken out of the building already, and she was the last one unaccounted for. For just a millisecond he hesitated, stunned by his reaction to her. He had to mentally shake himself to clear the lust burning in his brain, and the smell of smoke stung his nose reminding him of where he was.

Turning quickly, he leapt forward, and just as his body reached the glass front door of the building, he felt and heard the groan of steel and creak of wood. The pressure of the collapse pushed him and his unconscious bundle out through the doorway, landing them about twelve feet down the sidewalk. The heat that blasted up his back brought tears to his eyes and knocked all the oxygen from his body. His lungs seemed to collapse into themselves, and the muscles in his shoulder where he had taken the brunt of the landing trying to protect her, were screaming at him.

In slow motion he rolled to the side to see if the woman was still alive under him. His heart jumped for joy when he saw her breasts rise and fall. They rose above her tank top, glorious swells of femininity that just looked like they needed to be set free. Someone helped to lift him to his feet, and he saw the EMTs putting her onto a stretcher as they pressed an oxygen mask to her face. They wheeled her quickly to a waiting ambulance, and she was gone.

Please, Please. Let her be okay, I can't lose her now.

"What the hell was that?" the sharp voice at his side was angry and confused.

Damon glanced toward his brother's dumbfounded stare. He realized that his twin had heard every word Damon was thinking as usual and didn't understand it one bit. Devin was almost his mirror image, and the only other person who shared all his quirks and vices. How could he explain to Devin what had just happened to him in those few seconds when he didn't completely understand it?

Bending over with his hands on his knees, trying to catch his breath, Damon did the only thing he could do.

She's my mate, he thought. He heard Devin's sharp intake of breath before they both headed for the hospital to find her.

CHAPTER TWO

"*A*re you sure, Damon? I mean there was a lot going on, and maybe all the smoke went to your brain." Devin had spent the last two hours pacing the waiting room at the hospital, trying to convince Damon that he had lost his mind, and needed to go home and forget about this woman. Nothing seemed to work, and Damon wasn't budging from the hard, plastic chair he sat on.

"Devin, I know you're the Alpha, but I'm asking you not to doubt my instincts. I need to see her; talk to her. She's my mate, and I felt it to the bone as soon as I got near her. What am I going to do now?" Damon looked so pained that Devin almost laughed.

"I guess you're just going to have to waltz into her hospital room and tell this tiny hero that you're a werewolf, and she smells yummy. After which we can follow it up with a visit from her new Alpha brother-in-law, and I will welcome her to the pack." Devin laughed so hard at the image that he had to sit down.

Damon just grimaced and slumped over with his elbows on his knees, his hands tangled in his thick black hair. He knew how crazy this whole thing sounded, but he wasn't letting her get away from him now that he had found her.

He'd already been through the emergency room himself to get checked out, because the fire chief wouldn't take his word for it that he was fine after that rough landing back at the scene. As a werewolf, his body healed incredibly fast, and by the time he was released, his pains had gone. The doctor that saw him reminded him how lucky he was that he made it out of the building at all—like he didn't already know it.

According to Devin, the decision had been made to just let the fire burn itself out, so there were only ashes left of the building now. Thankfully everyone that was inside before the fire was accounted for, and had escaped serious injury. Only the last three people pulled out needed to go to the hospital to get looked at.

His mind flashed back to the moment that he saw the first woman rolling down the stairs as he and the other guys were going back into the building to search one last time. As they reached the first one, a second woman had bounced down the steps to the floor, but she had held the small child, who was obviously out cold in her arms. For that couple of seconds the team's plan to rescue the victims seemed to be working perfectly. They had found them, and they were alive, but then he had picked her up.

Damon came back to the present with the scent of his mate still filling his nostrils. It seemed to simmer in his brain, making everything but being near her seem unimportant. Just then a doctor came into the waiting room and stopped in front of the men.

"Are you the family of Caroline Trainor?" he asked in a soft voice.

"No—" Devin started.

"Yes!" Damon jumped to his feet, determined to get information from this doctor no matter what lies he had to tell him.

The doctor hesitated, looking from one man to the other. "Are you her husband?"

"Not exactly, ummm, I mean, uhhh…" Damon wasn't sure where he was going with this, but he knew that he had to see his woman.

"What he means is that they are engaged, but not married yet." Leave it to Devin to come to the rescue, and give him the right words.

The brothers locked eyes and shared a silent agreement to get what they were here for. Damon breathed a sigh of relief as the doctor nodded and continued.

"I'm sorry. I didn't realize that Caroline was engaged. I'm Dr. Lou Jackson." The doctor shook hands with both of the men. "I'm the doctor assigned to her. Caroline has some smoke inhalation, but is otherwise fine. She will have bruises because of the fall down the steps, but we couldn't find any other injuries. She hasn't regained consciousness, although we expect her to anytime. I'm absolutely amazed that a woman her size was able to help two people out of that fire without more injury." He stood still, shaking his head with a slight smile on his face, until he realized that the men in front of him were impatiently waiting. "Would you like to go back and see her now?"

Devin and Damon followed the doctor down the sterile hospital hallway. Damon could hear his brother in his mind as they walked.

What if you're losing it, little brother?

Just wait! She will feel the need to mate when she sees me. And then we can take her home, and I will claim her as soon as possible.

Damon had never really seen either one of them settling down. He had always pictured them as forever bachelors, loving the ladies and enjoying their freedom together. They liked the setup that they had. Devin was the Alpha of the pack, and was capable of facing any danger with Damon as his second. They were surrounded by their closest friends and pack members at the firehouse, and the rest were a few miles outside of town at the den. They worked hard, and played harder, so how was a mate going to fit into his world?

Nuts. Taking a mate at this stage in your life is nuts, Damon.

Damon threw a backward glare at him over his shoulder at Devin's input. Devin just smiled, acknowledging that his brother meant no disrespect. Damon knew that, if asked, Devin would do everything in his power to help him, and to make her transition to wolf easier.

As they reached the doorway of a room, the doctor slipped the chart in his hands into the file holder on the door and said, "Be patient. Your fiancée has been through quite an ordeal and may need some time to readjust. We're going to keep her here overnight for observation, and then we will let her go home." He stumbled for a moment like he just couldn't find the right words. She didn't have a home after the fire had destroyed the apartment building. "I mean, well, we will discharge her tomorrow."

Damon nodded at him in silent understanding and shook his hand again. "Don't worry. I will take care of her."

Turning away as the doctor walked away back down the hallway, he reached for the door handle, but Devin stopped him with a hand on his shoulder.

"You know that if she IS your mate, there is no turning back?" Devin stared into his identical twin's eyes, and took a breath. Whatever he saw made him drop his hand, and shrug. Damon hoped that meant he understood his need to go to his mate, and then together the brothers pushed through the door and past a privacy curtain.

His eyes burned as he stared at her lying in the hospital bed surrounded by machines that beeped out her heartbeat and pushed air into her nose. All the breath left his lungs for the third time that night, and he froze.

She was stunning. Her soft mahogany-colored hair was thick and wavy, but was currently pulled up in a terrible ponytail on top of her head. Her skin was a golden-caramel color, but currently much paler than it should be, making the faint freckles that dotted the bridge of her tiny nose that much more prominent. Her face was a heart shape that ended in a soft point at her chin, and her eyebrows were perfectly sculpted arches above her mile-long eyelashes. Her lips were slightly too large to balance her other features, but damn they sure were a pretty soft-pink color, and just begged to be kissed.

Perfect was the word that came to Damon's mind as he ate up the vision of his destiny. She was about five foot four and considering he had already held her in his arms he knew she couldn't weigh in at more than 115 pounds. She had felt curvy in his arms, and her breasts were fairly large on her petite frame. Her hands were small, but her fingers were long and feminine. He frowned when he saw her finger nails, because where they were probably once delicately manicured, now they were chipped, broken, and had soot underneath them.

Reality rushed through his brain like ice water. His woman had almost given her life to save a neighbor and her six-year-old son from a burning building. Damon felt pride fill his chest that this angel could be his true mate. He wanted to scoop her up in his arms and shake her until she told him why she had risked her life, and then kiss her until she promised to never do something so dangerous again.

Damon turned around, realizing his brother hadn't said anything since they came into the room. He found Devin standing in the doorway looking like he had seen a ghost.

She's my mate, too.

Damon growled under his breath as he heard the thought from Devin clear as day in his mind. "What?"

"I don't understand it either, Damon, but she's my mate. I smell her, and feel her here," he whispered, and then Devin put his hand on his chest over his heart. "She was born for us, and she will accept both of us as her mates."

"That can't be! What are you talking about? I don't want to share my mate." Damon's mind raced as he struggled to grasp what was happening. He knew that twins were a special case when it came to werewolves and mating. More often than not they would end up with one mate for the pair of them, but now that Damon had found her, he just didn't particularly want to have to share her. Not even with his Alpha twin brother!

His wolf came angrily to the surface, and he could feel his claws just under his human skin aching to break free and tear his brother's tongue out for even daring to look at his woman. And then he saw the connection. It was in Devin's face and in the tension in his muscles. Damon accepted it in that moment. He accepted that his Alpha brother also had a claim on this woman, but he sure as hell didn't know how they were going to make Caroline accept it.

The beautiful woman in question suddenly took a deep breath, moaning loudly, before opening her eyes. The blank stare of her soft chocolate-brown eyes told the brothers that she hadn't yet completely become aware of her surroundings, so they waited silently as she got her bearings. Damon stood as still as possible, staring at his mate with a powerful need to protect and comfort her. He could sense Devin just behind him to his left, tense and on edge as his wolf fought to come forward and claim its mate.

When she focused in on Damon, a small wrinkle appeared between her brows, and questions filled her eyes. He could sense her disorientation, and wanted her to read the answers in his eyes, but being human and not wolf, this was an unrealistic hope. Her intense gaze ate him up. Slowly her eyes drifted down from his dark hair past his muscular chest, lean hips, and all the way to his booted feet and back up to meet his dark, ivy-green eyes. His wolf growled in his head at the interest he saw in her eyes when they met his.

"Hey, beautiful, I'm glad to see you're awake." He smiled his most charming smile, flashing the dimple in his right cheek at her, and moved closer to her side. He just barely kept from reaching out to touch her or hold her hand, but somehow he just knew that his woman wouldn't appreciate it just yet.

Caroline was so confused. This wasn't her apartment, and it wasn't the hospital staff room, so where was she? She tried to focus in on her surroundings only to have her stomach tighten when she saw the stranger next to her.

"Who…who are you?" She winced at the pain in her throat and the rough sound of her voice as she tried to scoot higher in the bed. Her muscles fought against her as she moved slowly. She felt like she had been bulldozed by a truck, and her vision blurred for just a moment.

Before the man next to her could respond, a movement at the door caught her attention. She jumped a little bit when a mirror image of the man on her left, moved up to her right and leaned in closer as if to hold her hand. She saw him take a deep breath in. Was he smelling her? He must like my perfume, she thought in confusion. She felt very small with the two large men standing over her bed. She assessed the two of them, her eyes jumping between them for a quick moment. They were tall, and they were built well. Damn were they ever built well. The one on her left had a deep dimple on his right cheek, and the one on her right had a deep dimple on his left cheek. Other than that, they were carbon copies of each other. Surely, she was dreaming them up.

"Shhhhh. Don't try to talk too much. You've had quite a day, and that throat has to be sore from all the smoke you swallowed," the second guy crooned softly to her. "We damn near lost you today, and we just can't figure out what were you thinking sticking around in that apartment."

Caroline closed her eyes as she remembered everything that had happened. The fire, the sounds, and smells raced through her brain, and her heart jumped into her throat. Her eyes popped wide open, and she gasped out loud, "Tyler? Molly? Are they okay? I have to see them."

Surprised by her outburst, the two men looked at each other, and seemed to be silently communicating before interrupting her panic.

"I'm guessing they would be the two lucky ones that you helped rescue today. They are absolutely fine, sugar, and are quietly resting in a hospital room a floor down from us in the pediatric unit. Apparently, mama bear wasn't willing to be in a separate hospital room from her cub. The little guy—Tyler—he had a struggle coming out of an asthma attack, but they have him stable now. He should be okay." Guy number two spoke softly to her. His voice was a soft caress and calmed her jumpiness immediately. He spoke to her as if he knew her intimately, but Caroline knew she had never seen these men in her life.

She damn well would have remembered them if she had. Working in a hospital as a nurse meant seeing all kinds of people, and occasionally patients formed an attachment to their nurse. She had been caught off guard by many people stopping her at Walmart, or the gas station hoping she would remember them from when they were patients. It was an inevitable part of her career.

To the best of her knowledge, she had never ever nursed any men that were built like Adonis, and as dark as Lucifer. Not to mention there was no way she would have forgotten those killer dimples that kept flashing as though they were waiting for her to do something special.

She closed her eyes, and took a couple of minutes to gather herself as the men continued to stare at her. The one on her left, guy number one, began to caress her hand softly as if she were a frightened animal.

"Who are you guys, and as much as I'm enjoying the company, why are you in my hospital room?" she finally asked, although she didn't really want to know because it might mean the end of the gentle touching. It had been years since she had last felt a man's soft caress, and she remembered now why she liked it.

"Well, beautiful, I'm the man that carried you from a burning building today. I'm Damon, and this is my twin brother." Guy number one seemed to be trying very hard to keep their interaction casual, but she sensed something more in the tightness of his muscles. It was almost like he was struggling very hard to resist something. He gripped her hand just a little tighter, but his fingers never stopped their lazy circles over her palm. The friction of his callused fingertips almost made her moan, and she blushed lightly when her mind wandered to what those fingers tips would feel like in other more intimate places.

She remained quiet, thinking about his huge arms holding her tightly at the apartment building when he scooped her up, and a sudden delicious heat filled her belly. Her insides quivered, and something inside of her ached to reach out, and grasp him by the hair so that she could just devour him whole. What would he taste like? She closed her eyes again, trying to get her mind to slow down, and process his words without the effects of his closeness. She opened her eyes and looked back at Damon closely. His name seemed to suit him, and she had to bite her tongue to stop herself from whispering it back to him. He was such a large man, and though Caroline had always been small, she had never felt so dainty as she did now staring up at him from her hospital bed. His emerald eyes flashed and filled with heat as his lips curved up in an arrogant grin. She could see his nostrils flare, and she felt her pussy weep with joy into her panties at that sinful smile. Oh, God, I'm horny after a near-death experience, she thought to herself.

"Hey, I'm Devin, and I'm hoping that you won't ask us to leave, sugar." The second godlike specimen reached up, and brushed a lock of her hair from her forehead, petting her hair like a small child. "You still look a little pale. Do you need us to get the nurse for you?"

"No, I'm fine. I'm just really foggy. I think I need a drink of water though. My throat feels like someone rubbed it with sandpaper." She scooted up and used the buttons on the hospital bed to raise the back so that she was sitting up more than reclining. It made her feel just a little bit more confident as she stared down these sexy brothers.

Both men reached for the pitcher of ice water left on the hospital cart. Damon held the cup as Devin poured the water, and they both waited with bated breath when she leaned forward to sip from the straw. Her eyes widened when she heard what she thought was growling coming from both of them as her lips went around the straw and sucked hard, but the cold water felt glorious to her parched throat, and drove all other thoughts from her brain for a moment. She closed her eyes and gently leaned back on the pillow with a large sigh. Opening just one eye a crack, she peered at the two of them leaning over her.

"How long do I have to stay here?" she asked them impatiently.

"The doctor said you could go home tomorrow," Damon said quietly. "But Caroline, the building is gone."

Tears were falling from her eyes before she even processed his actual words. The realization that she had no home hit her. Everything she owned was gone! She thought of her photo albums that contained the only pictures of her parents she had kept after they died, and the embroidered bed pillow that her grandmother had made. She thought of all the things that weren't just things to her, but were gone forever.

How was she going to start over? She had barely been surviving, and now she had nothing.

She felt strong arms reach for her, and pull her up from the bed. One of the brothers settled in behind her with her leaning back against his chest, just holding her as she sobbed, while the other shushed her by stroking her hip and back trying to help soothe her. There was nothing sexual in the motions, and yet her skin burned under their soft touches. She wasn't used to such affectionate concern for her, and it made the pain in her chest that much more raw. She cried until she had no more tears in her, and her head hurt from the emotional exertion. Then she got irritated with herself.

Caroline Trainor was not a crier. Even when her parents died on September 11th, she spent the next several months stoically focused on what steps she needed to take to clean up what she could of the lives they left behind. She spent weeks arguing with bill collectors about whether or not her parents were actually dead, because she didn't have their bodies to prove it. They had worked on the ninety-fifth floor of the North Tower in the World Trade Center for an insurance company. Every day they shared a cab to work, and had spent their lunch hour together for more than twenty years. The first hijacked plane crashed into their floor, and Caroline knew almost immediately that they were dead, even before the towers actually fell. She just felt their loss deep down to her core, like they took the light out of her soul with them. Almost eleven years later, Caroline still didn't have any bodies to prove their deaths, and she would never have them, but she did have bills as proof that they once existed.

She mentally shook herself when she realized that her silence was causing more tension then her tears had, and when she lifted her head to see the man that was holding her close, her eyes met Devin's intense light-green orbs, and lust filled her belly again. A surge of electricity seemed to shoot from his hand on her scalp all the way through to her clit. It hummed with interest, and she took a quick breath in, biting her lip to keep from moaning. She felt his arms tighten just slightly as his muscular body clenched. His fingers moved to the back of her neck, softly massaging the tension there. It was like he knew what her thoughts were!

What was she doing? She had just been through hell and back, and all she could think about was the way this man's muscular chest and rock-hard abs felt against her breasts in this flimsy hospital gown. He smelled divine, like cedar and coffee, and she wanted to lick his dimple just to see if he tasted as good as he smelled. She blushed at her own lewd fantasies, and pulled herself away from his grip. Instantly she felt a sense of loss when they broke contact. Surely that wasn't possible, that she could crave a stranger's touch? She had obviously just gone too long without a man, she thought, and forced herself to keep the distance between them.

Devin could feel her pull back, and he wondered what caused her resistance. He could smell the desire on her, and he had thought that she wanted to kiss him just a moment ago. He had held himself back, hoping she would make the first move. He didn't want to rush her, but damn, he wanted her so much. He could afford to be generous with her for the moment because of the trauma she had just been through, but his wolf struggled inside of him at the nearness of its mate. Soon, he assured himself, she would allow fate to take over, and they would join.

His eyes met Damon's as he let her retreat a few more inches from him.

How do we tell her?

We don't. Not now. We need to give her some time to trust us, otherwise we will scare her. I'm not backing off, Damon, just giving her some space to accept it.

I'm not going to let her go, damn it. I know she's my mate, and my wolf needs her. This will work out. It just has to.

"Umm, thank you, for rescuing me. I…uh…I think I need to rest, but I appreciate you guys comforting me. I'm not usually so emotional. Do you do this for all the ladies you pull from burning buildings?"

Caroline scooted farther away from the wall of Devin's chest, and he moved off of the bed to let her lay back against the pillows again. She quickly pulled the covers up over her breasts, but not before Devin noticed her hardened nipples and rapid breathing. His cock twitched against his zipper, and he wanted desperately to whip the blanket off of her and show her how good they could make her feel.

Damon chuckled as he watched her settling herself again, and grabbed her hand to bring it to his lips. "Nope. Only you, beautiful. Do you have any family members we should call so that they don't worry about you? The fire is all over the ten o'clock news."

She shook her head and looked away from him. In doing so, it brought her face-to-face with Devin, and for a moment he could see the loneliness in her eyes as she admitted she had no one to call. Devin's heart broke for her, and he wondered what had happened to make her so lonely. He wanted to bring a light to her eyes just to see if they sparkled when she laughed.

"Okay, then we will have to figure out what you will need when you leave here tomorrow, so that we can go shopping for you. I'm not exactly sure what the hospital did with the clothes you were wearing when you came in." Devin could hear that his tone was bossy, but he couldn't pull off nonchalance like Damon. He just felt too much.

"I don't need anything. I'm not sure what I'm going to do, but I'm sure you guys have done more than enough. You don't have to help me. I will be fine from here. I'm actually a nurse here at this hospital in the emergency room, so I have friends here. Thank you both." She seemed to be dismissing them both as she withdrew her tingling hand from Damon's large one.

Caroline pulled her hand away from the big man's grasp, and even without his touch, she felt the sparks of heat on her skin. She looked up after a second and made eye contact again with Devin. Those eyes could surely see right through her!

"That's not up to you, sugar. Damon and I are going to help you one way or another, so get used to the idea. Tomorrow you can come home with us, and we will get you settled and back on your feet in no time." Devin said it in such a demanding way that a shiver of excitement caused goose bumps on Caroline's arms. She loved the authority in his voice, and it crossed her mind that he might be that kind of strong man in bed, too. She had always preferred a lover that was just on the dominating side, but she didn't like to be pushed around too much. She was a grown woman who'd been taking care of herself for the last thirty years. There wasn't a chance in hell she was letting this strange man tell her what to do and where to go, no matter how delicious he and his brother were.

She started shaking her head at him. "What do you mean I'll go home with you? I don't even know you. Why do you think I would go home with you?" She was getting herself worked up with irritation, and the flush in her cheeks caused both men's nostrils to flare. Her eyes widened in surprise and then narrowed with anger as Damon said one phrase: "Because you're ours."

Astonishing herself, Caroline started to laugh loudly. She was almost giddy with the hilarity of his statement. Why would this man that she had never met, possibly think that she would just agree to whatever demands he made of her? Why would she be attracted to that kind of a possessive statement? She shook off the brief flash of heat that she felt, because secretly she knew that she was attracted to it. Something inside of her knew that she couldn't let him know that yet, or she would never get any control back. She had heard of arrogance, but Lord have mercy these men took the cake!

She could tell that these two overly large men didn't find the situation nearly as humorous as she did, so she struggled to regain her composure before meeting Damon's irritated gaze. Chin thrust defiantly in the air, she clearly said, "Not a chance, darlin'."

CHAPTER THREE

Caroline lay in her hospital bed contemplating the scene that had played here earlier. After Damon laid his claim, she'd jerked back from him laughing almost hysterically. Once her giggles passed, she had gotten pissed. Devin tried hard to calm her down and explain the situation, but all Caroline understood was that for some reason both of these men felt some sort of obligation to her and wanted her to just go along with them. Well she was not some whore that just picked up strangers and had ménage a trois with them for shits and giggles.

She had asked them to leave her alone, and Damon had angrily stated that under no circumstances would they ever leave her alone again. Devin quickly agreed with his brother, but seeing her mutinous glare, he seemed to realize that they were pushing her too hard, so he dragged Damon out the door with a promise to her that they wouldn't be far. Right now they were sitting outside the hospital room in those silly hard plastic chairs guarding her door. Or at least that was what her friend and nurse, Tina, told her when she came into the room to check Caroline's vitals. Caroline could tell that Tina was desperate to know who the men were, and why they were sticking so close to her, but she didn't ask. For that Caroline was grateful. She didn't know the answers to the questions in Tina's eyes, and she wasn't sure she was ready to face them yet. She did know that she felt safe with these two men, and in her gut she knew that she needed to explore her reaction to them. She fought her own pride at being ordered around, and having her life "handled" for her, but she knew logically that she didn't have many options.

She had no family to call, and very few friends that she was comfortable asking to help her. She needed a place to stay, and according to Devin, they had an extra bedroom at their home with a separate bathroom. He said that they usually rented the room out or let friends use it, but seeing as how it was currently empty, they would happily let her use it. But why would strangers let her live in their home for free? What did they want from her?

She felt her face flush again at the lascivious thoughts that filled her brain whenever she asked herself that question. She could see in their eyes what they wanted from her, and she wanted it as much as they did, but she was determined to prove that stubborn Damon wrong. She was no man's possession.

Caroline had called Molly and Tyler's hospital room, and Molly assured her that they were doing wonderfully. She told Caroline that she had already spoken with her sister in Denver, and she was coming to Kansas City tomorrow to load them up and take them to her house until they could get back on their feet. She cut the conversation short when Molly started to cry and thanked her for saving their lives. In Caroline's mind she hadn't done anything that anyone else wouldn't have done, but she knew better in her heart. She had almost died saving Molly and Tyler.

As she thought about everything that had happened, Caroline heard the brothers' gruff voices outside arguing with another voice that was softer, but definitely male. She leaned forward to try and see around the privacy curtain that blocked the doorway. Just then her coworker, Carter Lawrence, came hurrying into the room followed very closely by an angry Devin, and an equally angry Damon. Clearly they were not happy to see Carter, but she smiled politely and reached her hand out to take the bouquet of daisies that he held.

"Caroline, I'm so glad to see you're okay! When I heard what happened and how close you came to dying..." he broke off and looked at her with so much emotion in his eyes that Caroline felt her heart break. She knew that Carter wanted her, and he had asked her out multiple times, but there was no spark with him. She saw him as a brother, not a lover.

The two thunderclouds standing next to the other side of her bed, however, caused her to clench her thighs as she caught another whiff of their masculine scent, and felt their dominating anger radiating out at this intruder. They looked dark and dangerous, and she couldn't help but feel her insides melt, and her heart race.

"Thank you, Carter. As you can see I'm just perfect, in fact Dr. Lou says I'll be out of here tomorrow. The flowers are lovely. What a sweet gesture!"

Carter grabbed her hand and held it close to his chest, and Caroline had to twist her arm back and forth to loosen his hold so that she could take her hand back. She rubbed it absently with her other hand, trying to soothe away the discomfort his touch brought her. It was odd how hot she got when one of the twins touched her, but Carter's touch just gave her creepy goose bumps. Although they remained alert with their arms crossed, both Devin and Damon seemed to relax slightly when she broke contact with Carter.

"I ummm, uhhh...well, I just wanted to check on you and see for myself that you were okay. It looks like you have plenty of help." Carter paused, glancing at the glowering faces of the two powerful men, and took a small step backward.

"That was really nice, but you didn't have to come all the way down here, Carter. Don't you work this evening in the ICU?" She was attempting to chat and distract him from the wall of intimidation that the brothers had become.

"Yeah I do, but I told Sara at the desk that I would be a little bit late so that I could come and see you. Do you need anything? You can stay at my place if you need to when they release you. I would be happy to have you." He sounded like a small puppy begging for his master not to kick him, just staring at her with some sort of crazy longing. Her bodyguards both growled again at his last statement, and his face turned a pale shade of green.

"Thank you, Carter, but I'm sure I will be okay. I haven't quite figured it all out, but I will let you know if I need anything, okay?" She said it as casually as possible, trying to figure out how to ease the tension in the room.

"You know I would do anything for you, Caroline, right?" His voice was quiet, but not quiet enough. She could tell the brothers heard him and knew his feelings for her.

"I know, ummm…I just prefer to keep my coworkers as coworkers. You know that, Carter. I appreciate the thought though. It's good to know that someone is worried about me." She saw the pain pass through his eyes when she dismissed his affection for her. She couldn't continue to let him believe there was a chance though, especially with the feelings that she had for the two men next to her. How she could possibly have feelings for two strangers, she had no idea, but she had to face the truth, and so did Carter.

As Carter stood silently on the left side of the bed, he was obviously determined to ignore the other men, and concentrate on her. She rolled her eyes, and set the flowers down on her bedside table. After crossing her arms across her chest, she decided to just address the elephant in the room—so to speak.

"Carter, this is Devin, and Damon…"

"Gray. Damon and Devin Gray," Damon said through his gritted teeth. Then he ground out in a quiet voice, "Who are you to Caroline?"

"I'm a friend." Carter put emphasis on the friend, and even Caroline could see the lust and longing in the small man's eyes. He had sweat on his brow, and his limp brown hair was cropped close to his scalp. Caroline would have to explain to the men at some point that Carter was not an intimate friend, but their jealousy struck a nerve inside of her, and it was obvious that Damon still wanted to force the point to Carter that he was staking his claim.

"Not anymore," Damon growled. His hands were now clenched at his sides, and his breathing had quickened. It almost looked like he was growing in size, as his anger became more obvious.

Carter grew pale and took a quick step backward. He seemed torn between wanting to run from the twins and wanting to step to her side and stand his ground. She could see his indecision, and she could damn well understand his confusion.

"*What?*" She gasped and stared at Damon. "Who do you think you are, just announcing that like you can decide for me? I don't even know you, you arrogant jerk!" Her face grew flushed with her fury, and she moved up onto her knees pulling the oxygen tube off her face and throwing it aside. The bouquet of flowers hit the floor as Carter bumped her bedside table as if he, too, was surprised by her fury.

Were these men all idiots, or just arrogant? Did they all think that a woman was a toy that they could own and use? Well they were about to learn the hard way that Caroline Trainor was no ordinary woman.

"I will not let you scare my friends off you...you...overgrown ogre! Carter came here to see me out of genuine concern and friendship, and he has as much right to be here as either of you two cavemen!" Her voice had gotten lower and tighter as she ground out her anger at them.

Damon reached out to her, trying to calm her. Instead it only infuriated her more, and she jerked away from him. These men were absolute strangers to her, and here Damon was intentionally trying to scare off a man much smaller than they were, as well as making the choice of her friends for her like they owned her.

Caroline glared at them complete silence, seething as she struggled to keep her frustration under control. Carter took that moment to reach over and kiss her on top of the forehead and wish her better. She tipped her head up so that his lips would have better access to her head, which caused Damon to give an exasperated grunt and stomp from the room.

Carter stared at Devin for just another moment as if he expected him to leave the room as well, but Devin stood like a gargoyle clearly not leaving him alone with Caroline.

"I guess I will just have to come back later to check on you. Please let me know if you change your mind about a place to stay, or if you just need anything. I mean it, Caroline. Anything at all." He headed to the door with one quick look back. His eyes took in the scene of Caroline damaged and weak in the hospital bed with her enormous guard dog Devin at her side, and she thought she saw a glint of anger in them. She shrugged it off. Surely she misread his intention. Then he flashed a tentative smile and waved as he left her room.

Devin put the flowers back on the table and then sat down in the chair next to Caroline's bed to watch his mate as she fought to control her temper. He watched her breasts thrust forward, the nipples hard points as anger pulsed through her. The flush on her high cheekbones was almost regal as she continued to glare at him, and at the door where the other two men had left. Up on her knees on the bed he saw every bit of her curvaceous body. She was magnificent, and he couldn't wait to see her passion when he held her beneath him and pushed himself inside of her.

Caroline stopped when there was no one left to grumble at, and slowly settled back down to rest on her heels. She glared at Devin and waited expectantly for an explanation.

"Are you done?" he asked in a soft voice trying to restrain his amusement. There was no reason to upset her more. He admired the way her light, caramel-colored skin glowed with her impatience, and a muscle ticked in her jawline.

He wondered how long it would take her to notice that she only wore a scrap of a hospital gown that wasn't even tied in the back, and it barely covered her breasts when she leaned forward. Her ponytail had fallen out, and her long, curling hair was wildly falling down past the top of her ass. She was magnificent when she was in a temper.

He saw on her face when she got her emotions back under control, and she settled down. "Why are you guys here, Devin?" she asked quietly. Easing herself back down onto the pillows, she pulled the blanket back over her lap, and laced her fingers on top of it.

Devin contemplated what to say, inwardly groaning when his brother gave in to his impatient frustration.

What's going on? Damon's voice sounded in his head.

She's calmed down and wants answers.

Tell her I'm sorry, man, I don't want her mad at me.

Damon, you just scared the hell out of her friend, and took away the chance we had to explain all this slowly.

I know, but I can't help it. I have to protect her.

Just shut up and wait outside, I will talk to her just give me a few minutes.

"As Damon indicated to your *friend*, he wants you, and I want you just as much. I can't explain everything now, but please trust me. We would never do anything to hurt you, and we will always be there to take care of you and protect you. We just get a bit overprotective." He smiled his most charming smile.

"How can you want me? You don't even know me. And why are you so determined to protect me?" She sounded heartbreakingly confused, but Devin knew that now wasn't the time for explanations. It would only succeed in making this situation harder.

He stood up and moved to her side, taking her hand and placing it on his chest, holding it against his heart.

"I told you I can't explain it all at the moment, but just know that I can feel my need for you deep inside of me." As he said it, he searched her eyes for some recognition of his soul. The mating bond was undeniable, and he could see her shiver at the unexpected intensity of his emotions. He knew this woman was meant for him, and he would not give her up, even if it meant sharing her with his brother. "Do you feel something when you look at me?"

"Sure, I'm attracted to you. I mean look at you. But I'm well past the age of letting lust rule my life, Devin. Sex doesn't equal stability, and that's what I want in my life. I need some logical answers and a plan for tomorrow."

"I don't mean lust, Caroline, but it's good to know you want me as much as I want you." He paused and watched the flush of heat rise in her cheeks and her breathing pick up. "I mean deep down, can you honestly tell me that you don't feel a connection?"

Caroline's hand rested on Devin's hard, muscular pec, and she could feel his steady heartbeat. She couldn't find any air in her lungs, and her voice wouldn't work, so she remained silent. As they stared at each other, her lips parted, and her eyes drifted over his face. With his high cheekbones and that square jaw, he looked like he was cut from a slab of granite. He had a strong nose, and it reminded her of a picture she once saw of a proud Native American warrior. Domineering and controlling, he was hard in all the right places and soft where a woman needed him to be. Her gaze reached his mouth. He had sensual lips that were fuller on bottom, and perfectly straight teeth. Her gaze held steady there until his lips turned up into a satisfied smirk. She had just enough time to think to herself *yes*, and his lips met hers in an explosive kiss.

She felt the struggle within him to keep his control as his lips explored hers. The kiss was possessive and demanding, but so soft she knew that she had the choice to stop it. To her surprise she didn't want to, and she melted into it. Her hand grasped a fistful of his shirt while his hand came up to hold her jaw. His tongue drifted softly across her bottom lip as she opened to him, and their tongues began to dance. Never had she experienced a kiss so powerful. She could feel him to the painted-pink tips of her toes, and she wanted to pull him into the bed with her and tear his clothes away. She wrapped her fingers tightly into her blanket, forcing herself to sit still and just enjoy his embrace.

Devin pulled back first, still holding her chin gently in his strong hand, and he stared into her eyes as he let out a sigh.

"Shit, sugar. That was intense. I knew you would taste good." He smiled that dimpled smile, and she almost smiled back.

The arrogance of the statement settled into her brain again like a cold tidal wave, and she jerked her head away from his grip. What was she doing? The smoke must have ruined her brain.

"Get out," she said softly, refusing to meet his eyes. "Please just go and leave me alone. I need to think." Devin looked stunned and stood silently for a few moments before he turned to the door.

"I will be outside if you need me, Caroline. We will talk more later, but believe me, we will finish this." He walked calmly from the room, and Caroline leaned back into her pillows and cried herself to sleep.

CHAPTER FOUR

*T*ina woke her from her slumber several hours later to check her vitals.

"You're awake!" She smiled at Caroline as she checked her blood pressure. Caroline couldn't resist smiling back at her closest friend. "How are you feeling?"

"I'm pretty sore right now. My lungs hurt, and my throat is raw." She reached for the ice water still sitting on her bedside table, and took several swallows.

"Yeah, tonight might be rough, but you should feel better by tomorrow. Your bruises won't heal very fast though, that one on your left hip had us worried when they brought you in. Thankfully the X-ray showed that it wasn't broken, just bruised." Tina chattered away as Caroline lifted her gown to look at the bruise in question. It was black and purple, and really did look bad. It must have come from her tumble down the stairs. She laid her head back against the bed as Tina shined a flashlight into her eyes and looked at her throat. Then she offered Caroline a pain pill and waited patiently as she swallowed it down.

"So, are Mr. Sexy and Mr. Damn Sexy good friends of yours that you never told me about? If so, why the hell didn't you tell me about them? They are sitting outside your door looking like guard dogs for now. And one of them told Dr. Lou he was your fiancé?" She sat on the edge of the bed and smiled conspiratorially at Caroline.

"Their names are Devin and Damon. I've never met them before today. They are firemen, and the one with the dimple on the right cheek is Damon—I think—anyway, he is the fireman that helped me out of the building. No, I am not seeing them, and I'm not sure why they would tell people we are engaged. Oh my God! I hope that doesn't get passed around the rumor mill. I'll have to talk to them and make sure they don't have the wrong impression. Anyways, how did you end up on this floor tonight?" She settled back into her pillows, enjoying the comfort of chatting with Tina.

"Dr. Lou owed me a favor, so I called it in tonight. I couldn't have my best friend in the hospital and *not* be her nurse, could I? Why wouldn't you want them to have the wrong impression? How could you not want to explore the possibilities?" Tina was clearly not interested in discussing her job and wanted the dirt on the brothers. Caroline sighed heavily and looked down at her fingers clenched in her lap.

"They say that they feel something for me. I guess they think it's like love at first sight or something? I'm sure they won't stick around much longer. They are pretty hot though, huh?" She shared a smile with her friend and licked her lips.

"Honey, if one of them even hinted at an interest in me, I would drop my panties and jump on him. I think you need to relax and enjoy the attention. Maybe I can have whichever one you decide you don't want?" Tina moved from the bed, patting Caroline's hand as she stood. "So, what are you going to do when you leave here tomorrow? The apartment building is toast. Where will you go?"

"I don't know yet. I guess a hotel." A teary sting filled Caroline's eyes for just a moment at the reminder that all her worldly possessions were gone.

"You could stay with me if you want to, but you will have to take the couch. The Red Cross might help you with the cost of the hotel if you prefer it." Caroline smiled at Tina, knowing that her offer was generous, but unrealistic. Tina lived in a tiny one-bedroom home that was barely enough space for her, much less a live-in guest.

"No, actually the guys offered to let me stay at their place in a spare room. I'm a little apprehensive about taking their offer though."

"*What?* Are you joking? Two sexpots rescue you from a burning building, fall madly in love with you, and now they want you to come and live with them—together? Have I just stepped into the twilight zone? Earth to Caroline. *Say yes!*" Caroline laughed out loud at Tina's outburst.

Tina was such an outgoing, carefree soul, and she always said what was on her mind without a filter, but Caroline knew that her friend had a softer, more self-conscious side to her. She didn't truly trust too many people, so she took it as a good sign that Tina was so easygoing with the twins. She couldn't help that she second-guessed her choices and tended to be more reserved. The two women balanced each other well, and had become fast friends when they met their first year of nursing school. Tina had been such a spot of sunshine in Caroline's dreary world that Caroline had quickly gravitated toward her, and thankfully Tina had helped to pull her further from her depression. They shared the bond of having both lost someone they dearly loved in a horrific tragedy, and they bonded over their grief. They considered each other best friends and yet the only time they seemed to spend together anymore was at work. Caroline made a mental note to herself to make plans to go out with Tina soon. She missed having a social life.

"Caroline? Are you all right? You seemed a long ways away for a minute there." Tina's brow had furrowed out of worry, and Caroline sighed again.

"I'm okay, Tina, and you're right. I need to take more chances. They seem like nice, respectable men, and they are firefighters. I think I will test the waters and agree to stay with them for a few days to get back on my feet. Maybe something will come from it. I haven't had a relationship in so long though, and I wonder if I would even remember what to do with them if I got them naked." Her face heated as she shared her thoughts out loud, and Tina licked her lips and smacked them in an air kiss.

"It's like riding a bike, sister. I'm sure you will manage!" She left the room, laughing loudly, and Caroline heard her pause at the doorway and say to the men. "Hi, I'm Caroline's best friend, Tina. Keep an eye on her for me, and tell me if she gets disagreeable, in *any* way."

Caroline couldn't hear the twins reply, but she groaned at the implications of Tina's comment. What was she getting herself into?

The next morning Caroline's friends from work filtered in and out of her room checking in on her. There were so many female visitors that she began to wonder if they were actually there to see her, or the man meat outside her hospital-room door. According to Tina several other firemen had visited the hospital, talking with her twins and then leaving. Why would the whole fire department seem to give a damn if she lived or died at this point? This whole situation was getting away from her.

She had a promise from her boss that her job was safe, but that he wanted her to take a couple of weeks off to recover and figure things out. She had several weeks of paid time off saved up that she had hoped to use for a vacation someday, so she could afford a little bit of time to herself.

Carter hadn't been back, and she was relieved. As much as she appreciated his concern, she also didn't want to lead him on. He was such a nice guy, and it was impossible not to feel bad for him. She also found that she enjoyed the spark of jealousy from the men when he was around, and it scared her.

As she lay in her hospital bed waiting on the charge nurse to bring her the discharge directions, and bill to sign, she thought again about Molly and Tyler. They were so dear to her, and she had no idea when she would see them again.

She had met the two of them four years ago when they were all moving into the apartment building over the same weekend. Molly, being a single mom with a two-year-old, was struggling to figure out how to simultaneously watch her energetic son, and unpack boxes that the moving company had dropped all over the apartment. Caroline had always wanted to have children of her own, but when her parents died, she realized that if she wanted a stable future, she needed a good income and a career. She settled for dreaming of personal stability instead of men and love, and it suited her just perfectly.

She had just enrolled in nursing school the year before they met, and the move to the apartment was intended to cut some of her expenses because she could walk to both school and the diner where she was waitressing her way through school.

She had offered to hang out in her free time with them, in order to help keep Tyler occupied, and a true friendship was born. From then on she spent every Friday evening babysitting Tyler for Molly, who had been waitressing at the same diner that Caroline once had. They had dinner together at least one night each week, and Caroline had even trusted Molly enough to share her dreams of a family with her. Molly was encouraging and wanted Caroline to date more often, even though she herself declared that one ex was enough to deal with and she had no desire to date until Tyler was at least out of college.

Caroline even spent last Christmas teaching Tyler how to roll the cookie dough to the proper thickness so that the sugar cookies were just soft enough, and then he had shown her how messy frosting cookies could actually be with a preschooler helping. Caroline enjoyed the feeling of family that she had when she was with them.

Now she was facing starting over without them around. Knowing Molly's financial situation, it was unlikely that she would be able to afford to move back to Kansas City after this. She would have to stay in Denver with her sister, and would probably just settle down there. Caroline would miss little Tyler more than she could bear to think about.

Lying in bed, dozing in and out and thinking through her history with Molly and Tyler, she felt a gentle breeze across her cheek. She knew one of the twins was in her room because she could smell him, and feel his heat. She opened her eyes to find Damon watching her apprehensively. His eyes seemed to light up when their gazes met, and she couldn't hold back her smile.

"Caroline, I'm sorry I was so hard on your friend last night. I didn't mean to upset you," he said to her quietly. It was so quiet that she almost wondered if he actually spoke it, or if she just heard his thoughts somehow.

"Thank you for that. You need to understand that I'm not yours to order around, Damon. I'm my own person, and I will make the decisions where my friends are concerned."

"I will try to control the urge to break his scrawny neck in the future." The laughter in his eyes calmed her jumping heartbeat as she realized that he was just teasing her.

"Good, I'm glad we have an understanding." She smiled back, unable to help it. She loved seeing how it made his face light up. God, he was such a sexy man. He was all rough edges, and a soft heart with an unusually deep-seated need to protect her. These two brothers were going to be her undoing. She could sense it.

"However…" He paused dramatically, waiting for her to focus her attention back on his eyes before speaking. "You are mine. Mine and Devin's. You will come to accept that, but I'm willing to give you more time to fall head over heels in love with me."

His smile was playful, but his words carried a strong message. She wasn't sure she liked his assumptions, but she didn't want to argue with him again. Settling for rolling her eyes at him, she noticed the shopping bag in his hand.

"What's that?" she asked.

"Leave it to a woman to sniff out new clothes." He chuckled. "The Red Cross worker that came in last night said that the hospital would have had to throw out the clothes you were wearing, so I went and got you some things to wear. Hopefully they fit. I had to ask your friend Tina what sizes I should get for you. She also said that your favorite color is purple, so…"

He looked so hopeful that she would be happy with his purchases that she couldn't help but smile wider. "Thank you. You didn't have to do that, you know. I appreciate that you and Devin want to help me, but..."

"I know, I know. You don't know us. That's okay, beautiful, we can slow down and give you time, but don't shut us out. Now, out of bed with you, let's see how they fit so that we can get you out of this place." He reached his hand out as if to help her stand, and she arched her brow at him, crossing her arms under her breasts.

"Damon. You will *not* be helping me change clothes. I will put them on, but you will wait outside while I shower and get dressed." She hoped the look on her face was serious enough for him to resist arguing, but she could feel her own laughter bubbling up. She liked this lighthearted, flirty side to him.

"You may not be strong enough to stand up and move around on your own, Caroline. Let me help you." He looked both concerned and devilish as he made his plea, but she wouldn't back down. She shook her head and pointed to the door, grinning.

"I will be fine. I've been dressing myself for thirty years now. Thank you for your offer." She smiled back at him.

"Fifteen minutes, beautiful, and then I come looking for you," he called out as he headed back to his chair in the hallway.

His easy laugh sent ripples of desire through her. How could these men have such an effect on her? She was such a sane woman, and she had never been so attracted to anyone. As she learned their different personalities, her desire for them increased, and it made her wonder if there wasn't something to their claim that she was fated to be with them. She shook her head at her own crazy thoughts and opened the shopping bag. Inside she found a pair of blue jeans, and a purple sweater as well as a pair of lacy purple panties with a matching push-up bra. At the bottom of the bag was a box with a pair of new tennis shoes and a pair of white socks, and last she found a small bag that contained toiletries for a shower.

Caroline almost cried at the thoughtfulness of this man. He had everything a girl would need, and had even gone shopping for it. She didn't think she had ever received clothing from a man in her life. Her one ex-boyfriend had not been big on gifts, so she wasn't used to accepting them. She had no chance against these men if they kept treating her like she was someone special.

She decided to ignore those feelings for now, and she headed for the bathroom that was attached to her room. All her muscles were screaming in pain. She turned the water on as hot as she could and gave a throaty sigh as she settled into its heat.

As she relaxed into the water, her mind alternated between images of the two men. Damon seemed to be so much more impulsive then Devin, but he was also the one that was more thoughtful of her needs. Devin was more serious, and could clearly keep his calm in the face of her temper. She felt Devin's desire to protect her even from a distance, and she could sense Damon's need to see her smile when he looked at her. The only physical differences were their dimples on opposing cheeks, and just slightly different-colored green eyes that made her want to purr when they looked deep into her. They were quite the puzzle, and she was determined to figure them out somehow, and to move at her own pace in this new relationship.

As she came out of the steamy shower, her head spun a bit. It seemed she wasn't quite as strong as she thought. She slid down the wall to sit naked on the floor with her head resting on her knees. Her vision blurred, and she felt nauseous. The previous day's events hit her again, and she started to tremble violently. She crawled across the tiles to the toilet and retched. Her stomach was empty, so she couldn't vomit, but her body seemed to want to get rid of all the pain from last night. Settling on the floor next to the toilet, curled in the fetal position and shivering, she knew she couldn't get herself back up to get dressed, and that scared her.

Just a second later, the door to the bathroom burst open, and both Devin and Damon stood there staring at her with fear on their identical faces as she broke down in shock on the floor of the hospital bathroom. She felt a quick rush of embarrassment, before she was wracked with a second wave of violent tremors. She clenched her eyes shut, trying to slow the spinning of the room and relax her breathing.

She felt one of them pick her up, as the other wrapped a towel around her, and they took her into the other room. Instead of sitting her down on the bed, she felt the twin carrying her settle into the plastic chair, and adjust her across his lap with his arms wrapped around her tightly. Her body shook hard enough to make her teeth chatter, and she couldn't seem to catch her breath. She looked up to see Damon holding her tightly while Devin stood inches away watching her. Damon rocked her back and forth for a few moments, until her body began to relax into his hold. She kept her cheek pressed against his hard chest, absorbing his strength. His arms around her felt like iron supports holding her together so that she didn't fall completely apart. It was wonderful.

"I'll go get the nurse," he said to his brother.

"No!" she gasped, and she pulled out of Damon's arms to stand. She had to grip the towel tightly to keep her dignity in front of them. "I'm...I'm okay, I promise. I just got really light-headed after my shower. My head was spinning, and it made me nauseous, so I had to sit down, and then everything just seemed to hit me all at once. My stomach is settling now. I just need to catch my breath for a minute. Oh God! I'm so embarrassed!" She used her free hand to cover her face as she blushed and prayed that they would take the hint and just get up and leave. Instead they stayed put, and again in the silent tension, she got the idea that they were communicating with each other.

"You shouldn't be embarrassed, Caroline. You've been through a lot." Devin's voice was close to her ear, and she felt that sizzle of need as it rumbled through her.

"Please let us help you," Damon added.

"Thank you for coming for me. I don't think I could have gotten up." She still covered her face with her hand, and her breath left her lungs in a shudder. Her wet hair dripped down her back, and her toes were getting cold now that she was coming back to reality.

She tightened the towel around her and ran for the bathroom. "Oh my God, I need to brush my teeth. I'm sure I have terrible breath right now." She heard the two men snicker as she quickly broke open the toothbrush on the counter, and after a couple of moments she returned to the room where they waited for her patiently.

She watched them both warily, but neither spoke. Their green eyes followed her nervous hand up to tighten at the opening of the towel, ensuring it stayed closed. "I guess I'll get dressed now. I can do that by myself I'm sure."

Damon stood up out of his chair, and their towering frames surrounded her. They had to stand at least a foot taller than her, and the muscular heat of their bodies was impossible to ignore.

Damon lifted her chin to look into her eyes, and he kissed her. It was the best first kiss—after the one she shared with Devin—of her entire life. It was a kiss that was hard and soft all at once. It seemed that she was an appetizer on a plate to be devoured by him. Her soul seemed to reach out to grab ahold of his, trying to hold on for the wild ride. She pulled her small frame up against his body, and with his hand, he pressed her pelvis against his obviously hard erection. She moaned into his mouth and let go of her towel to grip his biceps. Her fingers curled around his hard, muscled arms, and her brain turned to mush. She couldn't think, and all she knew was this was where she wanted to stay. His tongue danced with hers playfully, and he nipped her bottom lip, drawing a soft moan from her as her pussy clenched.

Behind her she heard Devin clear his throat. His voice came out tight and almost sounded angry.

"Enough, Damon! Give her some breathing room."

As Damon pulled back from her, she felt the towel slip, and he reached out to grab it to protect her modesty. As his fingers skimmed the top of her breasts, her knees weakened and she stumbled. Four strong hands helped her to sit back down on the edge of the bed, and then silently Devin retrieved her bag of clothing from the bathroom and set it next to her.

"Are you sure you don't need any help, sugar?" he asked her, watching her carefully. Afraid to speak and beg them to touch her, she just shook her head and reached for the bag.

After another long pause, the two men each kissed the top of her head and then quietly left the room. It was several minutes before Caroline managed to put herself back together. She was now more determined than ever to get her answers from Devin and Damon. She had just realized that she craved them both desperately.

CHAPTER FIVE

"*I*t's only a few minutes away from here," Damon reassured Caroline as he settled her into the front seat of his mustang. "We will get you home and comfortable so that you can relax."

She smiled at him because he seemed almost clumsy as he tried to help her buckle her seat belt.

"Damon, I can handle my own seat belt. I'm not broken," she said in what she hoped was a firm voice, and he looked up at her.

"I know, beautiful, but then you wouldn't let me get this close to you," he said, his eyes drifting to her breasts.

"That's what you think," she muttered, and then her eyes widened when she realized she had spoken out loud. His breath caught, and his pupils dilated when he processed her words. Instead of speaking, he laughed and kissed her on the nose, stepping back from her car door.

She took a deep breath and chided herself for thinking out loud before she turned to wave good-bye to Tina who still stood on the sidewalk.

"Caro, call me and let me know how you are doing, or if you need anything. Take care of her, fellas. She needs some TLC right now. I will call you in a few days to check in and see how you're feeling.

Maybe you will be ready to jump back on that bike, and take it for a ride?" Tina smiled wickedly at her, and then at the twins who grinned back. Caroline shook her head and smiled to herself with the warm affection she felt for her friend as she went back into the hospital. Fidgeting in her seat, she watched as Damon hurried around the car. He stopped to say something to Devin, who waited next to them in a huge black pickup truck to follow the two of them home.

Home? Caroline wasn't sure she wanted to think about that, and what it meant. For now she was going along with their plan for her to use their spare room, but she intended to make other arrangements as soon as possible. She just didn't know how, or with what money she was going to start her life over. Being an emergency room nurse paid the bills, but the student loan debt that she carried was immense. She was stuck between a rock and a hard place…or in this case a stunning piece of man candy, and his identical twin brother.

She turned to look at Damon as he drove her home, and wondered to herself what kind of a man takes a strange woman home with no promises? What kind of man declares a woman his the day that he meets her? And what kind of a man is willing to share a woman with his brother? She wanted desperately to ask, but her gut told her she wasn't ready for the answers yet. Still, she would have to have this conversation soon, because she knew her future depended on the answers.

"You okay, beautiful?" Damon looked over to catch her staring at him, and flashed her a confident smile. "We can order something in for dinner tonight, pizza or Chinese, whichever you like? Or we can go out to dinner if you feel up to it. Devin and I don't cook, so I won't scare you off by suggesting that." He laughed out loud, and she couldn't help but giggle, too.

These guys sure were sure of themselves.

"Thanks. Pizza sounds perfect, and a cold beer if you have it," she said hesitantly, and looked back out to the road. *Why do I feel so shy around him? I'm never shy with men.* She hated the feeling of arguing with herself.

"Damn, I knew you were my kind of woman," Damon said, and reached over to caress Caroline's knee. He felt her tense a little, and the fragrance of her arousal hit him in the gut. He couldn't stop the low growl that came out of his throat. She wanted him, and he needed her. She just needed to trust him and Devin enough to give in. Damon knew he needed to claim his mate, and soon, or he might lose his mind to lust. Patience was never his strong suit. Devin could flirt with the best of them, and he loved to be the dominant in his relationships, but Damon was all heart and wanted to please his lover as much as possible. Sure, he flirted just like his brother, but in a more casual way. He loved to just have a good time, and keep things rolling. Finding his mate was a wonderful but completely unsettling dilemma.

Damon couldn't wrap his brain around how it was going to work to share Caroline, or how they were going to tell her their secret. How would she take the news that her mates were werewolves, and that they needed to make love to her, in order to claim her as theirs? Would she run screaming into the night, or would she embrace it like he hoped? What if she just plain didn't want them? What would he do if she tried to leave? Shaking himself mentally, he told himself he wasn't going to even consider that she might. This had to work out.

"Thank you, Damon. For letting me stay at your place for a few days. I really do appreciate it," Caroline said quietly.

"Beautiful, there is no thanks necessary, other than me thanking you for giving us a chance to help you." Damon wanted to argue with her, about her *few days* comment, but knew it would do no good. He needed to show her that he and Devin meant forever when they asked her to stay with them. "Are you doing okay? Hurting at all?"

"I'm sore, but okay. That bruise on my hip hurts the most. They gave me some pain pills at the hospital just in case I need them." She rubbed her hip as though thinking about it made it ache more, and her gaze drifted to the passing landscape. Damon wasn't sure what else to say to ease her mind. She seemed tense, and he hated that she was uncomfortable.

"Do you and Devin do everything together?"

"Mostly. We are very close, and like hanging out. You would think I would get tired of his serious ass, but I don't. He is my best friend. We work the same shift at the station, so we're usually off at the same time. We share the same friends, and interests for the most part, so we end up spending a lot of time with each other. We are twins after all. They say there is a unique bond between twins." He paused and glanced over at her to judge her reaction, and when she didn't respond, he went on. "Do you have any siblings?"

"No, I'm an only child. My mom had a tough time during my birth, and my dad didn't want her to go through it again. It bothered me when I was young, but I got over it. Tina is like a sister to me, and Molly and Tyler were close enough to be my family. How long have you guys been firemen?" she asked. Damon felt a spear of heat in his gut when he looked over at her and she smiled at him. That smile could stop traffic.

"Since we got out of school. That's all I ever wanted to be growing up, and it keeps us close to home and our family. Why? Do you like firemen?" His tone changed as he spoke, and his voice got slightly more playful. He wiggled his eyebrows at her, and Caroline gave a quick laugh.

"What red-blooded woman hasn't fantasized about a hot fireman? All that strength and masculinity wrapped up in a uniform..." She tapped her chin with her index finger as if she were deep in thought over a difficult puzzle.

"Beautiful, I promise you I will help you fulfill whatever wicked fantasies you have about firemen, and then we can make some new ones." He moved his hand in a firmer caress higher up her thigh, and let his hot gaze drift over her.

Caroline shivered slightly under his scrutiny, and then she flipped her long hair over her shoulder in a nonchalant gesture. "Promises,

promises. I don't make promises I can't keep, and you shouldn't either."

"I don't. And this is one promise I can't wait to keep." He laughed when her eyes widened just a bit. It was the only crack in her otherwise solid armor, but he could tell that he was getting to her. He couldn't wait to get her home.

~

Caroline quieted after Damon's last statement, trying to keep her body in control. She wished he wouldn't say things like that because it made it harder for her not to kiss the breath out of him. Her body was revolting against her, and she wanted to let go and just enjoy the ride, but her type-A personality was fighting the reaction.

She watched Devin's large black pickup truck behind them as they drove, and couldn't help but grin at how perfectly the vehicle matched his personality. Strong, dependable, and oh so masculine. Damon's dark-blue mustang seemed to fit him just as smoothly, with speed and flash, and a definite sex appeal. As she watched Devin following them, she noticed that there seemed to be another vehicle following him. This one was a white SUV with tinted windows, and there were definitely a couple of people in it. Why would someone be following them from the hospital? She blinked and laughed internally. Now she was imagining a stalker? It was probably just a coincidence that that vehicle was following the same path. She couldn't keep her eyes from straying to that SUV though as they reached the twins' home, and she watched it pass behind them slowly as if continuing on to their destination. Her puzzled thoughts were broken as they parked, and she got her first glimpse of her temporary home.

It was a pretty little ranch-style house that had a beautifully mani-cured lawn, and a cute iron bench on the small front porch. Small, neatly kept flower boxes holding red and yellow geraniums hung from the front windows, and four glorious rosebushes were blooming along the front walk. It was lovely, and gave her a sense of peace about coming to stay with these guys. Axe murders weren't flower gardeners, right?

Devin reached her car door as Damon shut off the ignition, and she blinked up at him. How did he get over here so fast? He held his hand out to her to help her stand, and his lips quirked up when he saw her tremble as she felt his touch again.

"This place is great! I love the flowers." She pulled away from him a step just to keep herself from running her hands over his perfect chest, and looked around.

"My secret hobby is gardening, but don't tell anyone. We wouldn't want to ruin my rep," he said, and she had to do a double take, because she thought she saw him flush as he shared this with her. She was surprised that this manly man would take the time to tenderly plant flowers and maintain them. It spun her opinions of him completely off track.

"Well, you obviously have hidden talents." She breathed out roughly, and immediately she felt herself become horny again as many other possible talents rushed her mind. *Stop it* right now, she told herself. *These men are just trying to be nice to you, and you will accept their hospitality without raping them.* She took a deep breath and marched forward up the walk.

Both men grinned at each other over her head as they moved toward the front door. They had noticed her struggling with herself. She was clearly horny, and they were enjoying every second of it. Devin walked behind her, watching her rounded ass sway as she moved. He loved the glints of gold and burgundy that flashed from her hair as it swept the top of her jeans. He couldn't wait to wrap his hands up in all that hair as he pressed against her ass, while she rode the hell out of Damon.

Wait. Where did that image come from? he thought to himself. He had never shared a woman with his brother before. Although they had slept with a few of the same women, it was never a ménage situation.

He was usually jealous of his partners and not much of a sharer, but for some reason the image of Damon fucking Caroline hard and fast slithered through his brain and turned his cock rock hard.

Cool it, Devin, I can't think if you keep planting those images in my brain.

Sorry. It's not like I can help it. You should see her ass in those jeans you bought her. I want my hands and cock in her so bad I can hardly stand it.

I feel your pain! Did you see how that shirt shows her tits? I had to bite my own tongue to keep from drooling on her in the car.

We have to control ourselves or we will push her away.

Damon could see Devin shake his head as if to clear his brain of the dirty thoughts. He, too, wanted to do sexy things to Caroline, but he had already pushed her too hard once, and he couldn't risk scaring her away.

They stepped into a bright foyer, and Caroline paused to look around her. There was a hallway to her left and a doorway to the right. A coat closet stood in front of her, and Devin stood directly behind her. She wished she could just relax into his heat as she stood there, but she forced herself to step to the side a few inches, putting space between them.

"Your room is this way, Caroline," Damon said over his shoulder as he led her down the hallway from the front door. He stood aside after opening the door at the end to let her go in first.

Caroline absorbed everything in the room as she entered it. It was simple with a queen-size bed that had an old quilt on it, and a tall wooden dresser next to what appeared to be a closet door. Both the bed and the dresser were a lovely dark wood, and looked like they were antiques. The quilt was obviously handmade, and just begged her to snuggle under it on the soft mattress. There was another door on the other side of the dresser that led to a small bathroom with a glass-enclosed shower. The two rooms were fairly undecorated, but the bathroom sported a set of luxurious white towels on the hooks that Caroline would swear were brand new. She could also see the edge of a pink bathrobe sticking out from behind the bathroom door where it was hung. The bedroom was as big as her whole apartment had been, and it was simply perfect. She visibly relaxed as she looked around, and then turned back to the men in the doorway.

They dominated the room, shrinking it in size just by being there. The air rushed from her chest. She could feel the edge of the bed at the back of her thighs and had to use every ounce of control to stay standing. She could sense that falling back onto the mattress would be an open invitation that she wasn't quite ready to make.

"Thank you, this will be wonderful." She gave them both a warm smile.

"I'm glad you like it. Damon hung a robe in the bathroom for you, and there are fresh towels when you want to take a shower." Devin watched her with an amused smile as she took in her new surroundings. She felt slightly awkward standing in a bedroom with two huge slabs of sexy man meat watching her and talking about buying her a robe and showering. Images of showering with both men swamped her brain and her knees grew shaky. "If there is anything else you find you need, let one of us know. We can take you over to the apartment building to see about your car tomorrow."

"Yeah, I will need to go to the mall and pick up some clothes, I guess. Now that I don't have anything left. My renter's insurance should cover some of that, I suppose. I need to call the insurance guy, too, huh?" Her voice was sad, and her hands trembled with emotion. Devin reached out and took her small hands in his and pulled her to him. Caroline let herself fall against his chest and rest her forehead there as his large hands stroked up and down her back.

"Don't worry so much, sugar, it's all going to work out. You've got Damon and I to help you. We can take you to get whatever you need tomorrow. But for now, you need to just relax and rest." His voice was low and took on a husky quality.

Caroline shivered, and he pressed her closer to him. She could feel the ripped muscles of his abs and chest against her breasts, and his scent enveloped her, muddying her senses. She felt Damon reach a hand out to pet her hair, and his fingers caught in the curls. The slight tug on her scalp as he pulled his hand away made her moan, and the two men froze briefly, watching her.

Gently, Damon wrapped his hand more tightly in her hair, and tugged until she lifted her face to look up at him. He brushed his lips gently across hers, and shuddered when she moaned against his mouth. Instead of deepening the kiss, he pulled back from her, and his gaze met Devin's. The two men stood with her between them, and Caroline could feel her thin strings of control ready to break.

Without even speaking, they both simultaneously pulled slightly away from her, and waited for her response. Irritation that they stopped, and then embarrassment that she didn't stop them herself stabbed through her. She could sense that if she said yes, they would make love to her, and her body wanted them too desperately, but she needed more time before she could let herself be in this kind of fling. She wanted a forever kind of love, and children. How would she do that with two men?

Caroline surveyed them both through heavy-lidded eyes, and grimaced. The bulges in their jeans told her that she was definitely not alone in this attraction. Surprisingly they both stayed quiet, just waiting for her next move. Once she had her own reaction under control, she struggled to grasp for words that would fit this situation. Oh hell, I just got here and I'm already letting them seduce me, she thought to herself. Squeezing her eyes shut to block out their heated gazes, she counted to ten, and then smiled again more confidently at them.

"How about that pizza and beer?" she said without moving a muscle. The reminder broke the sexual tension, and they all breathed again.

"You got it, beautiful." Damon chuckled. Reaching out, he grabbed her hand, pulling her away from Devin's loose embrace and down the hallway.

At the end of the corridor, they entered an oversized great room that had an open kitchen with a breakfast bar. It was obviously intended for entertaining a large group of people, but where a dining table should have sat at the back of the room, instead there was a poker table. It was covered in paper plates, cups, and the remnants of some recent poker night. To the right of the poker table was a massive sectional couch that faced an enormous big-screen TV. The couch was bare of pillows, and she noticed the walls were bare of any art, pictures, or knickknacks. There were two leather recliners that lined up perfectly for viewing that TV, and had a table with a lamp between them, but that was the extent of the furnishings. It was a bachelor's pad for sure.

The kitchen behind her was barren, which proved Damon's statement about their lack of cooking skills, and Caroline's urge to get in there and cook something took her breath away. She desperately had a need to cook for her men and take care of them.

What the hell? Her men? When did they become her men? Caroline put her hand to her temple, trying to rub away this crazy possessive feeling.

"Caroline, are you okay? Is the house not okay? What's wrong, sugar?" Both men stood before her with concern in their eyes. And was that fear on their faces?

"I'm good, just tired, and I got a little light-headed. I just need to eat something and maybe sit down." She moved to the couch and let herself get swallowed up in the overstuffed cushions. This is heaven, she thought as she kicked off the tennis shoes she wore and tucked her legs up under her.

She caught them smiling at her, and she blushed.

"Ummm, are we going to get some food, or can I least get a beer while you stand there staring at me?" They both jerked back to reality, and while Damon called for pizza, Devin headed for the fridge.

"So what do you guys usually do on a Friday night?" she asked as she took the ice-cold bottle from Devin who had already popped the top for her. She took a big swig of it, enjoying the feeling of the icy beer sliding down her throat, and then looked at Devin expectantly.

His eyes were suddenly like glowing emeralds watching her swallow the beer, and she wondered if he was picturing her swallowing him. He met her hesitant gaze, and flashing his dimple at her, he settled himself onto the couch next to her. He sat close enough to touch her thigh and rest his hand on it. He seemed to feel a need to touch her constantly. His fingers stroked her through the denim in lazy figure eights, and he took a deep breath before he answered.

"Usually Friday night we go out to a bar or club, or whatever if we're not working. Depends on our schedule. Working at the firehouse in twenty-four-hour shifts means that we can't plan too far ahead. Sometimes, we will go visit family just outside of town. What about you, sugar, what do you do on a Friday night for fun?" He watched her, almost like a predator watches his prey right before he pounces, but she tried to relax and just open up to him. She wanted to open up to them, which was unusual for her.

"I'm a homebody, so I don't go out too much. Most Friday nights I would babysit Tyler for Molly so that she could work an extra shift at the restaurant she waitressed at." She paused to keep herself from tearing up while talking about them. "I guess I will have to find new entertainment for Fridays now."

"Gotcha covered. Just let me entertain you, Caroline, I promise you will enjoy it." Damon tumbled over the back of the couch to lay next to her with his head on her lap. He wiggled his eyebrows at her, and she laughed at his dimpled, charming smile.

"Really? I'm sure I will be just fine entertaining myself, thank you very much," she responded, laughing.

"Why do for yourself what someone else is willing to do for you?" he asked.

"What if I can do it better myself?" she asked. She was flirting with him, and enjoying it immensely. The double meaning of their banter was not lost on her, and she wondered for the millionth time what it would feel like to have both of them loving her.

"Then I guess you would just have to let me sit back and watch so that I would know what you liked," he countered, and her breathing hitched. She liked this playful side to him, and she let herself reach out and stroke his cheek. His eyes closed, and he clenched his jaw. Startled that he wouldn't want her touch, she yanked her hand back.

"I'm sorry, Damon, I didn't mean to, ummm…I think I will go freshen up while we wait for the pizza." She tried to jump up from the couch, and Devin stepped in front of her while Damon turned his face into her without lifting his head so that she couldn't move. His eyes were in line with her breasts, and she felt her nipples harden at the close proximity of his mouth to them. He zeroed in on them quickly, and she watched his tongue dart out to lick his lips. She looked up at Devin to see the painful desire written on his face. She wanted these men, but she was scared.

"I don't know what to do here, guys. I'm new to this. I'm not even sure what *this* is?" She closed her eyes tightly and rubbed her fingertips against her temple again. Trying to calm her heart and her physical reaction to Damon's hot breath against her breasts, she slowly lifted her gaze, meeting first Damon's deep-green eyes, and then Devin's lighter green ones.

Damon moved his head away from her luscious breasts, and he sat up to face her directly. Devin knelt in front of her with his hands on her knees, and stared into her eyes.

"Don't run away, beautiful. I definitely want you, and I love you touching me." Damon sounded sincere, and she wanted to believe him, but she was so unsure of herself with these men.

"Caroline, we need to talk, and explain some things to you before this goes any further. But we need you to promise to keep an open mind and not freak out. Can you do that, sugar?" Devin asked her with such sincerity, and the pleading in his voice had her nodding her head. His hands were hot on her legs, and even though he didn't move, her skin was prickling with desire. His words frightened her a little bit, but she wanted to hear what he had to say.

"When Damon rescued you, when he first picked you up and held you, he knew you were meant to be his mate. It's fate that you belong to him, and he can sense it in his soul. Amazingly when I walked into your hospital room with him, I knew that you were my mate also. "

Devin spoke directly to her soul as he stared into her eyes, and the tension in the two men was suffocating as they waited for her response.

"Do you mean like love at first sight? You thought you loved me when you saw me?" she asked them warily. "That's sweet, guys, but…"

Devin gave a slight grunt and interrupted her. "Sort of, but not exactly. More like soul mates, but I hope we will learn to love each other." The vibration of his voice, paired with the heat their two bodies so close to her, brought back that foggy feeling in her brain.

"You don't know me, and I don't know you. I feel something for you both, but that's lust, or maybe it's the pain meds they gave me. I don't know." She paused, and then said, "Why do you keep calling me your mate? I'm not an animal." She turned her head to ask Damon, her lips just inches from his.

"No, beautiful, you're not an animal, but we are. Devin and I are werewolves." Damon paused for her reaction, but she just stared silently at him.

"Like sprout-fur, howl-at-the-moon, and eat-humans werewolves?" Her wary gaze went back and forth between the two men, and her muscles braced to flee when he continued to talk.

"Caroline, we are human, but not completely. We share our blood with the wolf, and wolves claim a mate for life. Werewolves don't eat humans, but I can't deny that I sprout fur and enjoy howling at the moon." Damon responded lightly, but Caroline kept quiet, processing everything they were telling her.

Her continued silence made him nervous, so Damon pushed forward. "We need you to want to be our mate as well, so that we can claim you. In our world a woman is protected and loved by her mate, as well as protects him and cares for him. It is something we take very seriously. In order to claim you, you must willingly claim us as well. The mating bond can't be created against someone's will. We must make love to you, and leave our mark on you."

She silently stared at him, and he wasn't sure what to do. He couldn't take the pleading tone out of his voice when he spoke next. "There is no other way. I can only promise we will go slow, and protect you from whatever your fears are."

Moments passed with no response to what he had told her, and finally Devin broke the silence. "Please say something, Caroline. We need to know what you're thinking."

Damon's wolf was struggling inside of him to get out and lay claim to this woman that was his mate. Her soft lilac fragrance drifted to his nose, and he watched his brother's hand clenching open and closed at his side like he was physically grasping for his control.

"I don't know what to say. I thought you guys were normal, and maybe even respectable. Now I'm scared that you're crazy, and you're trying to make me crazy, too. I'm in a home with two strange men I met yesterday after I almost died in a burning building, and they think they are werewolves, and I'm their mate. Now they want me to agree to let them fuck me, because they think they need to *mark* me in some way? I think I'm losing my mind! You two really need to work on your pick-up lines." She started to giggle nervously, and the more she giggled the more it began to sound like sobs. Suddenly she broke down, and huge sobs wracked her small frame as she struggled to breathe through them.

We should have waited. Damon glared at Devin while they both tried to console Caroline without scaring her more. Devin had his arms wrapped around her shaking shoulders, and Damon had his arm around her waist with his chin on top of her head.

We can't wait, and you know it. She wants us almost as much as we want her, and if we fuck her without her knowing the truth she will hate us. She has to choose us, or we can't have her.

I know, but I'm not sure I could let her go.

The doorbell rang, and Damon pulled away to get the pizza, leaving her clutching tightly to his brother as she sobbed. By the time he got back to the kitchen and set up plates and napkins, her sobs had turned to sniffles, and she watched him cautiously move around the kitchen. She pulled away from Devin, and he reluctantly let her go so that he could go to the kitchen to help Damon. They had to give her space, but they weren't sure what else to do with themselves.

∾

Watching them move around the kitchen, Caroline immediately missed their closeness, and found herself getting up from the couch and following to be closer to them. As she moved around the breakfast bar, the brothers reached for her. Maybe they could sense her need for their touch, or maybe they just felt the same need to touch her? She decided she really didn't care what the reason was as Damon wrapped his arms around her with her head on his shoulder, hugging her close, and she felt Devin cuddle up to her back with his hands resting on her shoulders and his nose in her hair. They stood there silently for several minutes before she broke the embrace.

"I want you. Both of you, so that part isn't the problem, but I need some time. Let me think on it for awhile, okay?" She saw the flash of uninhibited joy go through Damon's eyes when he heard her and had to stop herself from laughing. This was serious, and they needed to understand that she wasn't just going to accept what they were telling her.

"We know that, sugar, and we want you to accept us willingly. When you are ready to talk more, just come to one of us, but until then, get used to having us around. We aren't leaving your side." Devin gently turned her around to face him while he spoke to her, and she could see the fear of rejection in his eyes followed quickly by a flash of possession. It heated her blood hearing him. She mentally fought her body's horny reaction to him, and tucked her hair behind her ears in a nervous gesture.

Refusing to meet his possessive stare, she reached for the pizza box on the counter and quickly asked, "So what kind of pizza did you get?"

"Being wolves, we aren't really into vegetables, so I ordered an all meat and a plain pepperoni. Is that okay?" Damon was already handing her a plate, and clearly wanted to hear her approval.

"That's perfect, thank you. I'm absolutely starving." She tentatively smiled at him and helped herself to two pieces of pizza.

They ate pizza together at the bar in companionable silence, and Caroline drank her beer, thinking to herself about what the men had told her. How could they think they were werewolves? Were they crazy or was she? She had to admit to herself that there were odd things about these men, outside of the fact that they wanted to share *her* with each other. When they kissed her their eyes always seemed to brighten, until it almost seemed that they were glowing. She had dismissed it before, but now…she just wasn't sure what to think.

Surely they were just joking with her or trying to scare her? *I'm a grown woman, and I don't want to play games,* she thought to herself. *Well, maybe I will just call their bluff then.*

"Show me," she said quietly.

"Caroline…" Damon started to shake his head no, but Devin stopped him with a hand on his shoulder.

"Are you sure?" he asked her, and she lifted her gaze to meet his.

"Yes. Show me. That way I can prove to myself if you're crazy or not. I won't accept it until I've seen it with my own eyes." She kept her voice and gaze steady, but she could feel her insides trembling with nerves. Now that she had actually asked, she wondered if she was really sure she wanted to see it.

Nodding, Devin stood up and pulled her over to the couch. After she settled into the seat, Damon sat next to her and took her hand as Devin moved to the middle of the living room. She watched intently to see what he was going to do. Before she knew it, he had taken off his shirt, and his hands moved to the buttons on his Levi's. Her breathing increased and desire filled her belly as her gaze ate up his tight abs and sculpted chest, following the trail of dark hair down to the top of the buttons on his jeans.

"Wha…what are you doing? I told you I want to see you change into a werewolf, not get naked!" she choked out the words, wondering if they were as husky out loud as they sounded to her ears.

"Caroline, I can't change with clothing on or I will tear them apart, so instead of ruining a good pair of jeans I'm going to remove them. Don't worry, sugar. I won't ever hurt you no matter what form I'm in." Devin spoke in a quiet voice, and his patient tone told her how important this moment was to him. She bit her lip as she watched him, wondering if he could sense her fear.

"Baby, you are going to have to stop looking at me like that or I won't be able to concentrate!" She blushed but couldn't look away as he quickly pushed his jeans and boxer briefs down his hips. He stood proudly in front of her, completely naked, and allowed her to drink her fill of him. Her lips parted, and her eyes glazed over. The strength in his long lean limbs was staggering. Every line of his body was muscled and tense. The notch at his hips, and the curve of that muscle that led to his groin was fascinating. She wanted to follow it with her tongue. His huge cock stood erect against his six-pack stomach, and her fingers tingled with the urge to reach out and stroke him. The golden coloring of his skin made him look devastatingly sexy, and his eyes glittered as their gazes connected.

Devin's human brain told him that he was pushing her too fast, and that she wouldn't be able to understand fully without more time, but his wolf was snarling at him to hurry. His mate needed to see him change in order to believe his words, and he wasn't going to let her down.

He could see in her hazy eyes how much she wanted his human form, but he needed her to accept his wolf form as well. He prayed to God in his head that this would work. If she ran he knew the rejection would tear his heart out.

For years he had imagined what it would be like when he met his mate, and he had always believed that his mate would already be a werewolf. Faced with a human mate, who had no real understanding of the creature he was, he faltered. His gut was knotted with tension. He wasn't sure if he was making the best choice, but he was making the only choice he could.

Taking a deep breath, he changed.

CHAPTER SIX

*C*aroline shrieked and jerked backward. Right where Devin had been standing, now a large black wolf stood. The wolf was absolutely still and clearly waiting for her to acknowledge it. It was beautiful, with a small white streak down the left side of its face where a dimple would have been. Staring back at her were Devin's glorious light-green eyes, but they now had a distinct glow. He was larger than she imagined a normal wolf would be, but then again she had never come face-to-face with a real-life wolf. There was a sexy elegance about the way he stood there while she stared at him, trying to accept what she had just seen. It was real because she had never taken her eyes off of him. The change wasn't a gradual thing like she had expected, but instead it happened in the blink of an eye. First Devin was there, strong and steady, and then he was on four paws, tense and alert. Slowly, he moved toward her. His movement somehow more graceful and powerful in this form.

His paws were larger than her hands, and his fur shown in the dim light of the evening sun that filtered through the windows. Without understanding why, Caroline knew she needed to touch him. She dropped to her knees next to the couch, and tentatively reached out her hand. The wolf dipped his head until her fingers rested on the fur at the back of his neck. She wrapped her fingers into the silky ebony, and breathed in. She could still smell Devin on this creature, and staring into his eyes, she knew. She knew she couldn't deny what she had seen, or that something inside of her was drawn to him even in this animal body. Slowly she laid her head on top of his furry back and rubbed her cheek against him. He was so deliciously soft, and she couldn't help thinking that she never wanted to let him go. She needed him, and Damon.

She glanced over at Damon to see him watching her with pleasure glowing in his deep-green eyes. She should be running for her life now that she knew the truth, but instead she was tightly holding this huge black wolf. Under her cheek she could feel the relief in his muscles and then his transition from beast back to man, and she found her cheek pressed against Devin's bare chest. His arms wrapped around her and brought her hard against him up onto her knees. Her mouth met his, and as his hot tongue stroked hers, she exploded with pent-up desire. She opened herself to him, kissing him with everything in her soul. Her body shook as she pressed it hard against him, and he shifted to meet her. He ground his erection against her belly, and she groaned into his mouth at the delicious tingles that swept over her.

She felt him pressing her backward onto the floor. The soft carpet underneath her gave way, and cradled her as she fell off the cliff and into this cloud of passion. She accepted his touch and kisses willingly, and felt her heart soar when Damon's hands joined Devin's. She could feel Damon pulling at her jeans, and she lifted her hips to help get them off faster. Her pussy was swollen with need, and her heart pounded in her chest as Devin lay against her, naked and hard. Her hands reached out to touch him everywhere. She needed to feel the masculinity of him and hold it against her.

The two men worked in tandem to strip her bare to their eyes. Damon pulled her panties over her hips and off her legs, causing Caroline to gasp at the cool air against her hot skin. Before she could relish those sensations, Devin was pulling her shirt off over her head and quickly flipped the front clasp of her bra open, so that he could lay claim to her breasts. As her breasts tumbled from the purple lace bra, she had a twinge of embarrassment under their heated gazes. Her nipples sharpened into hard nubs and pointed directly at them, beckoning them to touch her. Weirded out by her body's instant reaction to them, she tried to reach up and cover herself as Damon stopped and stripped his clothes off in record time, but Devin growled.

"Don't ever hide yourself from us, sweetheart. You are perfect, and you belong to us." His voice was husky and filled with passion.

She dropped her hands away, so that they could indulge in a long look. She could see on their faces how much they desired her, and she squirmed under their hot gaze. Devin bent and kissed the large bruise over her hip gently, and then within a breath, Damon was kissing his way up her naked leg, stroking and teasing his way from bottom to top. When he reached her hip he, too, brushed a soft kiss over her bruise before moving on to explore her body. Devin suckled at her nipples. They tingled from all the delicious touches, and she pressed her body even closer to him.

Devin's hands caressed her face, back, and everywhere he could reach as he played with her tits. Her blood was boiling, and the tight, warm ball of need in her stomach was about to make her scream. She wanted to feel them filling her, and taking her. She needed their strength and hardness, and something inside of her yearned for more than just this sexual encounter, but she didn't know what more was. He stopped and lifted up to look into her eyes. Damon's lips were kissing their way across her upper thigh, but he, too, paused to look at her face when Devin spoke.

"Are you sure this is what you want, sugar? We can stop if it's not. It might kill us, but we will stop if you say so." Both men waited with bated breath to hear her response. They were all three wrapped tightly together and completely naked, but she could sense that they would accede to her wishes no matter what.

"Devin, if you two stop now, I will kill you, even if you are werewolves," she gritted out through her teeth, and she reached out to grab him, pulling him up from where he rested by her hips. She pulled his thick cock into her hand, stroking the velvet-covered shaft, and enjoying his soft growl. She wasn't very experienced with sex, but she knew that he was extremely well-endowed in his human form, and she wondered how he would fit inside her. The thought of his thickness filling her completely was dizzying, and she felt her skin flush hotter.

Hearing his gasp for air as she stroked her hand over him, she smiled and relished in the power her touch had over these men. They needed her as much as she needed them. She reached for Damon as he removed all his clothes. Holding both of them in her hands, she stroked their cocks while they stroked her body. She arched against Devin, as Damon's fingers found her wet entrance, and he slid one finger into her. Devin's mouth went back to licking and nipping at her nipples. He bit down a little less than gently on one and grinned to himself as she moaned in delight.

"You are so damn hot, Caroline." The strength of Damon's passionate words made her heart race faster as his voice rumbled across her skin. She arched up again, pressing her need toward the two men.

Encouraged, Damon pulled her thighs farther apart so that he could see all of her wet femininity. She was a natural brunette and kept her bush neatly trimmed, but not shaved completely. He loved the sight of her juice glistening on her curls between her inner thighs, and using his fingers, he spread her slick pussy lips to look at her swollen clit. She was moaning, and she smelled so amazing. He flicked his fingertip across her clit, causing her to rock up to meet his waiting tongue, and his wolf growled deep within him as he proceeded to love her cunt. She tasted sweeter than any candy he had ever experienced. He could go on tonguing her for the rest of his days if she would let him, just enjoying her taste, and her moans and cries of pleasure. He slipped a finger into her hot entrance and curled it upward until he found that tiny rough patch that was so sensitive inside of her. She squealed and tightened her fist on Devin's cock.

"Fuck, that's sexy." Devin leaned back to get a look at what Damon was doing to her.

Damon's fingers plunged deep inside Caroline's pussy, bringing her closer and closer to the edge. He never thought he would be comfortable watching his woman get loved by his brother, but this was almost too hot for him to handle.

Devin moved closer to Caroline's head and stroked her cheek with his finger, silently asking permission. His huge cock was inches from her face. She knew what he wanted, and before he could move again, she licked his thick length, tasting his salty flavor. The taste of him combined with the flick of Damon's tongue on her clit was driving her wild. Before she could question herself, she sucked his cock all the way to the back of her throat. The hot ring of her lips sealed around his cock, and he groaned back. She proceeded to suck him off, and he closed his eyes to enjoy it. She matched her soft licks to the ones that Damon was stroking over her clit, and it electrified her. She reached underneath to stroke his balls, and relished the grasping growl from his chest when he couldn't hold back his pleasure at the motion.

"God damn, that's good." He groaned loudly.

Damon, hearing his brother's tight groan, looked up to see Caroline sucking his dick, and their eyes met. He winked at her as his tongue wiggled softly against her, and his fingers curled to stroke her deeply. Her cheeks heated until she was sure they were pink, but she continued to suckle on Devin. Her eyes were half closed, as she bobbed on his cock, and she looked away from Damon only to catch Devin's hot gaze as he watched her.

Damon started pumping his fingers into her tight opening, and he slipped his other hand under her ass to hold her close. He used his lips to massage her swollen bud in a circular motion, gentle at first and then stronger and faster. She arched hard, and her pussy creamed when he pressed his thumb against her pink rosebud. She had never been touched there, and it brought another powerful wave of desire forward. He left his thumb just barely pressing into her ass as he suckled, and finger fucked her cunt.

Caroline loved the control she had over Devin's pleasure, but Damon's fast fingers kept her in constant fever. She wanted to be fucked. She bucked her hips up and increased her suction on Devin. Somehow the look in her eyes told Devin that she had had enough teasing, and he eased out of her mouth at the same time as Damon brought her to a white-hot orgasm with his tongue and touch.

Devin just watched as the orgasmic ripples went through her body, and he growled again when he heard her scream out Damon's name. He watched a satisfied smirk light up Damon's face, and took his challenge.

Devin was willing to share Caroline, but he needed to hear his own name on her lips when she climaxed. As Damon moved away from her sopping-wet pussy, Devin moved between her legs, and lined his hard cock up with her. He stroked the tip of his cock up and down her slit, reveling in her tremors and the fluttering of her pussy muscles against his tip.

"Please." She groaned.

"Please what, sugar?" he asked demandingly. She looked like a goddess with her face flushed, and her lips swollen from sucking his cock. His balls ached with need.

"Fuck me!" she moaned.

"Oh I will, and so will Damon. We will fuck you over and over again, until you never even dream of leaving us." With that he slowly sunk his cock into her tight pussy, feeling her muscles gripping him and pulling deeper and deeper. She screamed as another orgasm hit her, and arched up off the floor, grasping at Devin's muscular shoulders.

He could feel her fingernails biting into his skin as he began a slow rhythm of thrusting deep into her warmth. She was hotter than anything he had ever felt in his life. He wasn't sure he would ever get enough of her.

With her head thrown back and her eyes mostly shut she was the picture of passionate bliss. There were tiny goose bumps prickling her skin, and when he brushed one hand over her abdomen to hold her in place her muscles twitched. She was relaxed and pliant, causing his balls to clench up tightly. He loved watching a woman receive pleasure, and this woman especially made him burn.

Caroline didn't even notice when Damon moved up next to her until he kissed her. She tasted her own juices on his tongue and decided that it was the hottest flavor she had ever tasted. His fingers plucked at her swollen nipples as his tongue licked deep inside her mouth. Pulling her lips away from his, she reached for his cock. He growled softly as she tugged him up toward her mouth.

Damon wasted no time in changing positions, angling his body so that she could suck his cock deep into her throat. His dick was slightly longer than Devin's but not quite as thick. They were both much larger than any man she had been with, and she loved the way they filled her up at both ends. Each time Devin pounded into her pussy, her throat muscles grabbed at Damon's cock.

Devin wrapped his large hands around her upper thighs and lifted her ass into the air so that she was resting on her upper shoulders. Devin's face was rapturous, and Caroline let go of Damon's cock to scream out his brother's name. Her body racked with tremors of pleasure. Her hand came back to grip the base of his dick tight with her passion. Just as her orgasm hit her, she felt Devin sink his canine teeth into her shoulder. She writhed and cried out underneath him as another orgasm hit her. Something inside of her sparked and burned white hot as it flowed through her veins.

It was Devin's right as the Alpha of their pack to claim her first, but it reached into Damon's gut and twisted his heart to see another claim on her. He had to make his own mark, and *now*.

Devin leaned down and kissed her deeply, and then licked her shoulder clean of the blood from his bite. Damon had to admit it looked so beautiful there that he could feel his cock growing even harder. Devin pulled back and rested a few feet away so that Damon could mark their mate, too. Then Damon moved around until he was lying between her legs, holding her close. He loved the way her full breasts pressed against his chest. He felt her rub up against him as he nuzzled her throat, nipping at her chin and neck. Using his cock, he stroked her sensitive pussy gently, just keeping her from relaxing out of the orgasm she had just had. Then he suddenly pulled her upward into his arms as he rested back on his heels. She was now straddling him with her inner thighs resting on the top of his thighs, and her pussy cradling his huge cock. They were face-to-face now with their bodies pressed tightly together, giving her much more control this way. She smiled at his growl and locked her legs tightly around his waist as his cock sunk balls deep into her. Her head fell backward, and her whimper was deep and pleading. He couldn't remember ever feeling so good and wanted to somehow to sink even deeper inside of her.

He reached up and pulled out the clip that held her hair so that all the long locks swirled around them, and he groaned deeply. Wrapping one hand into her hair, and banding his other arm around her waist, they rocked like that, with Damon gently stroking her back up to the top of the crest.

"Oh my God, Damon, you feel so good!" She whimpered as her body started rippling around him, and his wolf preened at the passionate declaration.

"Come on, beautiful, come for me." He tugged at her hair until she tipped her head backward, and he could reach her neck easily. He nibbled and tasted her skin, memorizing every curve of her throat and shoulder.

She rolled her hips against him, trying to get him to move faster. He could sense her need, and using his own strength, pushed their momentum faster and fucked deeper into her. Just as she felt her soul break into a million pieces, he bit down on her shoulder opposite where his brother had left his mark. The bite sent her into oblivion. Whether she understood it or not she was theirs, body and soul. She quickly drifted off to sleep, cradled on the floor between the two huge men.

Hours later Caroline awoke still clutched to Damon's chest with Devin spooned up against her back. They still lay between the coffee table and the couch. One of them had pulled a blanket up over them, and her head was pillowed on Devin's broad bicep. She relished the warm security of their bodies, and wondered how long this could possibly last. She was ashamed that she had welcomed them both so easily, and hadn't tried to stop this whole situation before it got out of hand. What was she doing? She was a grown-ass woman who had a life, and responsibilities, and no desire to be owned by anyone. But she did want to be cherished, and she wanted desperately to be loved. When Devin had kissed her, she had seen a spark of something more than desire in his eyes, but she denied it to herself.

She could feel their even breathing, and when she shifted her weight, rolling off of Damon's chest and closer to Devin, she could feel Devin's hand slide gently over her hip, adjusting to her body and molding himself against her. It sent her blood pressure sky-high, and she had to clench her hands to keep from reaching back and grabbing for him. Every movement was glorious agony, and she craved more of them.

She finally decided that she needed to move away so that she could think clearly, and she gently pulled out from between them, standing above them at their feet. She admired them as they slept, wishing that just once everything would work out to a happily ever after. They were so tall and muscular, and damn! Had she ever seen abs so ripped in her life? Her mouth drooled as she envisioned following that line of muscles with her tongue, and hearing her men moan in pleasure again. Her men? Brushing her long hair out of her face, she headed for her room to shower and go to bed, alone.

She took a longer shower than she had anticipated, but her muscles were slightly sore after the loving she had just experienced. When she got out of the shower, she stood in front of the mirror looking her body over, and wondering what these two werewolves saw in her that made them believe she was their mate. She had been told by men in the past that she was hot, but like most women she saw flaws where others saw perfection. She knew that she had great breasts, and her waist was small, but her hips were nowhere near slim. She had an apple-shaped butt that ran into long, muscular legs. She wasn't really tall, but thanks to her daily yoga regimen, she was muscled and fit. She sometimes felt like her legs were too muscular, and looked too masculine. She just didn't think they fit the proportions of the rest of her body. Her face shape was often compared to Reese Witherspoon who she thought was lovely, but she had always hated her pointy chin, and wide forehead. Right now, with her lips swollen from kisses, she felt feminine, and she loved the warm, well-loved feeling her body had.

I can't stay here, she thought to herself. She knew that they wanted her, but the reality of the situation was that two men just didn't share a woman for a long-term relationship. Even if they were not completely human, they still lived in a human world, and had to fit into it. Two men with one woman was definitely not the socially acceptable everyday relationship. Shaking her head at her own thoughts in the mirror, she huffed and decided she would think more about all this in the morning.

As she stepped out of the bathroom, she found both men in her room. Devin stood leaning against the wall next to the bedroom door with his arms crossed, still completely naked and looking dangerously sexy. Damon sat naked on the edge of the bed, leaned over with his elbows on his knees watching her for her next move.

"Why did you leave us, beautiful?" he asked hesitantly.

"Ummm…look guys, I uhhh…that was great, well, really it was fantastic, and I really like you both, but uhhh…I ummm…" She stuttered and fumbled, holding her arms tightly around her stomach which had started to tumble as soon as she had opened the bathroom door and seen them. Devin pushed off of the wall and stalked toward her, his green eyes flashing, and his jaw muscles clenching. The way his powerful muscles clenched and relaxed with each movement would have made any woman wet, and she definitely was.

"You will never leave us again without telling one of us where you are going, Caroline. Is that clear?" His tone said that this was not the time to argue with him about ownership, and truly she was just too tired at this point to want to do battle with them.

She sighed and looked deep into his eyes. "Okay. Now what?" Do I turn into a werewolf as soon as the moon rises, or will I start growing fur? Do I become your flavor of the week that waits around for you to find another girl to fuck when you tell her she is your mate?"

Devin's eyes hardened in anger at her vicious words, but she couldn't hold it in. She was irritated, and there was an edge of fear in her voice. As if sensing his brother's temper was at the breaking point, Damon got up and reached out, pulling her away from Devin, closer to the bed.

"Now, nothing. Now we are going to lie down in this bed and get some sleep. We can talk about it in the morning. You have had way too much to process all at once. Devin sounds scary, but he really just wants you to know that we were worried when we realized you were missing from us. We want you close so that we can protect you. That's all." He pulled her onto the bed and tucked her in against him, spooning up against her backside. His fingers brushed her hair back out of her face, and he rubbed his face in the soft locks.

"Protect me from what?" she asked.

"Go to sleep, Caroline. We can talk more tomorrow." Damon's response was a soft mumble next to her ear, and it sent goose bumps across her skin. Caroline could feel him relaxing against her, and he sighed a contented sigh behind her.

She watched Devin walk over to the light switch to flip it off, and in the dim light of the room, she could see him head for the bed. He slid into the sheets, and lay there tensely as if unsure what he wanted to do next.

Although the logical part of her brain said that she should avoid him because she was angry with him, she couldn't stop herself from reaching out and laying her hand on his hard stomach. She wanted, no, she needed to touch him, and she relished the feeling of his ripped muscles as they fluttered under her palm. His skin was smooth and soft under her caressing palm, and she forced herself to just relax her hand, leaving it resting possessively over his abdomen. This was clearly the right move for him, because he scooted closer until they were touching. Facing her, he rested his large hand on her thigh, and pulled her leg up over his until her knee brushed lightly against his groin. He left one hand wrapped around her upper thigh, and he rested his chin on top of her head close to where Damon's was tucked into the back of her neck, nuzzling her hair. His other hand he brought up to hold her hand tight to his chest, refusing to let her pull it away. Caroline could feel the warmth of the brothers weakening her defenses again, and she slipped into the best sleep of her life.

Caroline's last conscious thought drifted into the twins' brains.

Mine.

Their eyes met as they heard her clearly in their heads, and they both grinned and held her just a little bit closer. Devin sighed in relief. The mating bond had taken, and now they would need to be patient and guide their mate into her new life as a werewolf. He knew that the next step was to explain the changes that would go through her body as she became a werewolf, and that scared him a little. He would also have to introduce her to the pack, but he wanted to keep her here for a few more days. Then they would share her with their family as the Alpha's mate. Finally, with a deep sigh he let himself relax into sleep.

CHAPTER SEVEN

a heavy knocking woke Caroline the next morning. It took her almost a full minute to clear her mind and remember where she was, and who was holding her captive in the bed. Devin's arm was like a manacle locked around her waist, but she shivered her pleasure at his hot breath on her neck, and his hard cock pressed to her backside. Damon was no longer with them, and Caroline could hear him talking with someone at the front door. His voice sounded impatient and irritated, and she could hear another man's voice arguing. She felt Devin sigh deeply behind her as if he realized that this intruder meant he would have to leave her warm and soft in the bed. For just a second he held her tighter in his embrace, and then he pulled away.

"I hate to let you go, but I have to go check it out. You better hit the shower, sugar, or else you won't get any hot water. Damon can spend hours in there." He kissed her forehead and rolled out of bed, leaving the room completely butt-ass naked. Surely he was going to his bedroom to get dressed. She hadn't seen where the guys' rooms were yet, but she couldn't believe he would want to greet anyone at the door naked. Although, she had to admit to herself that she would be a hell of a happy woman to have that hot body open any door to her.

I'm depraved, she thought. *I have spent all night with two men that are insane, and want to make me insane, too. I need to find somewhere else to stay soon or I'm not sure I will ever be able to leave.*

She headed to the bathroom to take another hot shower. The soreness in her muscles from last night had changed to just stiffness, and the steamy water relaxed and rejuvenated her. Not finding her clothes anywhere in either room, it dawned on her that they were probably still spread all over the living room where the guys stripped them off of her. So she pulled on the expensive-looking, pale-pink robe that hung on a hook in the bathroom. It hung on her, dragging on the floor because she was so short, and she giggled, quietly imagining that she probably looked ridiculous, but she damn well wasn't wandering the house nude like Devin.

She poked her head out the bedroom door. She could hear the men talking quietly, but the tone of their voices was still very anxious. She decided to take a chance and just head into the great room to see who was here. As she walked into the sun-filled room, she was surprised to see not just one visitor, but three.

Damon and Devin stood in the kitchen—thankfully they had both pulled on jeans—talking across the breakfast bar to three of the five hottest men she had ever seen in her life. Tall like the brothers, they ranged in size and build, but they all shared the same sexy chiseled jaw, high cheekbones, and bronzed skin. Five sets of eyes fixated on her as soon as she stepped into the room, and she almost swallowed her tongue in embarrassment. The newcomers were grinning at her like they knew exactly what she had spent the night doing, and each one took the time to grace her figure with an appraising look. No one seemed to find her lacking even with the ridiculously big robe on, and instead they all had an amused and curious glint to their smirks. She felt herself flush under their gaze, and pulled the flaps of the robe a little tighter to her breasts.

"Well aren't you a fine piece of a..." the one on the left started to say with a cocky grin, but Devin snarled at him, stepping toward him. She saw the stranger take a quick step back, bowing his head in submission, and her eyes widened at the response. The man in question winked at her as he met her startled eyes, so she relaxed a bit and smiled back. Damon moved over to her, and put his arm around her shoulders. He drew her tightly against his body, and then urged her closer to the imposing group to begin the introductions.

"Caroline, this is Liam, Cash, and Owen. Guys, this is Caroline Trainor. Our mate." He said it with so much possession and pride in his voice that Caroline tipped her head back to gape at him even as all three strangers gasped. Apparently this was a surprising situation to them as well. As she tried to figure out just how she felt about his possessive statement, she saw the look of love and pride in the ivy-green eyes that stared into hers. How could she deny him when she felt the same way? Swallowing hard, she felt her head spin just a bit as she looked back at the three men.

"No shittin'?" The one that had just spoken looked stunned, and now he was looking at her with a look of admiration and respect. He was tall, but not quite as tall as the others, only topping out around six foot or so. He was muscular, but in a fit, healthy and not-overly-concerned-with-working-out kind of way. His dark hair was cropped close to his head in a military-style cut, and he had a diamond stud in his left ear, and a gold hoop in his right eyebrow. His ice-blue eyes seemed to glow at her as they appraised each other. His T-shirt said Aerosmith and fit him like a second skin tucked into his dark-black jeans, and he wore black boots that looked like they belonged in combat. She could see he had a tattoo on his shoulder as well, but could only see the bottom which was a banner that held the word *Daphne*. He was a deliciously dangerous-looking man.

He caught her staring as he looked his fill at her, and he wiggled his eyebrows while his mouth turned up in an even bigger grin. That flirtatious smile of his could stop traffic, she thought. He was stopped again by the twins as they growled and even bared their teeth at him. He lifted his hands in front of him in apology, like he knew he had crossed an invisible line. Caroline paled and stepped backward away from

Damon's arm, but was stopped short by one of the other men speaking to her.

"Ignore Liam, sweetheart. He forgets his manners sometimes around normal people. Devin, you know he meant no harm. Caroline, I'm Owen, and this is my brother, Cash." He indicated the third man who had taken a seat on the right, and continued to stare at her with narrowed eyes and a cocky grin on his face.

Cash had that sexy-cowboy look to him. He looked like he had just rolled out of bed and stuck his cowboy hat on his head instead of running a comb through his curly black hair. He wore boots and faded blue jeans held up by a large silver wolf's head belt buckle. Caroline thought to herself that she had never seen a more perfect man for the cover of a country western album. All long, lean muscles, and his skin a shade darker than the other four guys. His face was covered in a five o'clock shadow that made his eyes a rich coffee brown, and she could see the laughter in them as he met her gaze. She could see that this one could give a woman a hell of a ride if he wanted to. Noting the warmth in his smile, she imagined he could also be a great friend if a woman needed him to be.

She turned back to survey the man who had introduced himself. Owen was the polar opposite of the other two rough-and-tumble men that he stood with. The tallest of them, he stood equal to her two men, and his body was just as muscular. He wore a button-down, sage-green shirt that was tucked into an expensive pair of gray dress slacks, and she could see his gray suit jacket hanging over the back of the bar chair he leaned on. His auburn hair was meticulously cut, and he was clean-shaven. All these details screamed money and power at her. His sex appeal was in classy sophistication, but his body under the clothes defi-nitely kicked her pulse into hyper speed. His hazel eyes looked almost gold, and reminded her of her conversation with the twins about their werewolf side. She knew instinctively that Owen was a wolf as well which in turn meant at least Cash was a wolf. She looked back to Liam and decided that this was probably not the best time to bring all that up again, and instead she decided to relax and have some fun with these men.

"You certainly don't look like a fireman." She blushed as she realized she had spoken the words out loud, but Owen just smiled back and shook his head.

"Oh, I'm a fireman, but only on a volunteer basis. I'm an attorney by day, and a superhero fireman by night." He tipped his chin at her, just daring her to comment on his career choice, but there was amusement in his eyes. Chuckling at his description of himself, she decided she liked these guys already, and relaxed her stance a bit more. They sure were a good-looking group. She couldn't help the dirty thoughts that seemed to flare in her mind.

Basking in the feeling of being surrounded by so much muscle, she greeted them. "Wonderful to meet you fellows. Are you friends of the boys?" Her voice was slightly husky with her arousal at being in the middle of a group of sexy men. She saw the flared nostrils as they all five reacted to her horny scent, and she felt her thighs become wet just thinking about the possibilities that this group had. She would put money on it that none of them had any problems finding a woman to warm their bed if they wanted one. *Just wait until I tell Tina about them,* she thought as she mentally shook herself to get her hormones back under control.

"Family, actually. We're all cousins. How did these two old dogs manage to find you, princess?" She could tell that Liam was now just trying to aggravate Devin, so she played along.

"They rescued me, actually. My very own knights in shining armor." She rolled her eyes to show her sarcasm and returned Liam's friendly grin to let him know she was in on the joke. Liam laughed loudly, and the other two men chuckled.

Devin moved possessively to her side, and, grabbing her hand, he led her around the breakfast bar into the living room. He sat down in one of the two matching recliners, pulling her onto his lap. She let out a feminine "eeep!" and he chuckled and started rubbing small circles on her upper thigh, which was now visible as the robe opened all the way up to her hip. She struggled to pull it back closed as she spotted her long-forgotten purple bra hanging from the lamp next to her. The heat in her face could have melted butter as she snatched it and tucked it quickly into the pocket of her robe. She couldn't bring herself to look at the other men in the room because she could sense that they had all seen her action and were silently laughing at her embarrassment. They had all followed into the living room and were now settling around the room. Cash straddled the arm of the sofa, while Owen stood with his hands braced on the back of it, and Liam lounged across it. Damon stood possessively behind her and Devin, and she felt his hand playing with her curly hair as she leaned back against Devin's chest.

"So, you're the one that kept them up at the hospital? We wondered what that was all about. You should be damn proud of yourself for saving that kid and his mom from the fire." Cash looked at her with a newfound respect as all the pieces to this puzzle clicked.

"I couldn't leave them behind. They are like family to me, and they are all I have left." Her formerly strong voice cracked with the wave of sadness that washed over her as she remembered that she probably wouldn't see her friends again.

"Not anymore. Tying your horse to these two mules, you have more family than you could ever imagine now!" Cash was laughing, but Caroline tensed and moved off of Devin's lap.

"That's where you're mistaken. I'm not tied to anyone, thank you very much. I need to go get dressed. Could someone drive me over to get my car from my apartment building?" She started to head back toward the bedroom, and Devin moved from the chair faster than she could blink to stand in front of her, with Damon slightly behind her.

She stood her ground, meeting his gaze defiantly. I will not be bullied, she thought to herself.

"Sugar, why don't you go ahead and get dressed and then we will talk more. Damon and I need to finish up with the guys, and then we will get them out of here." He brought his hands up to her shoulders, and she shivered as his thumb caressed the line of her jaw while he spoke quietly. Damon moved up next to Devin, and they both watched her closely.

"Aww, Dev, we don't have anything else to do for the day, why don't you let us spend a little time getting to know Caroline. I mean, it's not every day our Alpha claims a mate." Clearly Cash assumed that she was accepting of the whole werewolf thing, because he spoke of it like it was no big deal. Caroline closed her eyes and took a big breath before she turned to look over at him. Her eyes met his, and then traveled to meet each man's gaze until she circled back to Devin and Damon.

She glared at Devin in confusion and anger until he stepped back a step.

"What does he mean, Devin?" she whispered. She knew the answer. She could sense it in the tightness of Devin's muscles. He didn't answer right away, and she backed up to glare at him. "Damn it, Devin, what is he talking about?"

"Not now, Caroline. We will talk in a few minutes when they leave." He was angry, but she knew it wasn't at her. He was angry at himself, and he didn't like losing control of a situation. Her nerves were threatening to break out in a flood of tears, as she pondered the meaning of Liam's careless comment.

"So now that you have *claimed* me, you think that you will control me as well? Fuck you, Devin. I'll find my way out the way I came in." She pushed past him and ran for the bedroom. She managed to slam the door and flip the lock before she collapsed on the bed in tears. She was sad, and furious, and heartbroken, and ashamed, and lost…

All she knew was that these men obviously felt that they had some control over her and what she did with her life now that she had spent a night fucking them. *I'll be damned if I'm going to play Suzy Homemaker for some crazy-ass men who think they are werewolves. Hell, they probably drugged me last night, and I hallucinated the whole thing.* Her emotional roller coaster finally slowed, and she let herself fall to pieces. She cried until her eyes drifted shut and her body shut down into a dreamless sleep.

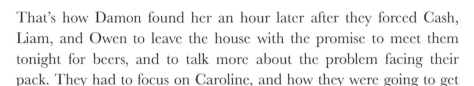

That's how Damon found her an hour later after they forced Cash, Liam, and Owen to leave the house with the promise to meet them tonight for beers, and to talk more about the problem facing their pack. They had to focus on Caroline, and how they were going to get her to listen to them.

Damon spent an hour pacing the hallway before he decided he had had enough of this silent war between Devin and Caroline, and he took the doorknob off of the bedroom door. He had told himself he was going to wait her out and make her come to him. After all that's what Devin was doing, sitting in the living room in silence, just waiting. Then he had started to think about all the reasons that she wasn't coming out and wasn't making any noise. He pictured her lying on the bathroom floor unconscious from a fall, or shivering sick on the bed having another attack of shock. And he made a decision based on the terror that filled his heart from his own imagination. He was going to kick the door in but decided that he didn't want to scare her any more than they already had, so he went and got his screwdriver and took off the doorknob to get to his woman.

She lay curled up on her side, her head on one pillow and the other pillow clutched tightly to her chest. Her face was swollen and tearstained, and her hair was spread out around her. Her robe was open with one long, smooth leg pulled up so that he could just see the curve of her ass peeking out of the opening. He moved across the room slowly, and settled down next to her on the bed. He pulled her into his arms, breathing in her scent and pressing against her back. She whimpered softly in her sleep, and Damon felt himself harden at the sound. She was so soft in his arms, and she fit against him like a glove.

Her reaction had hurt him, and it frustrated him that she wasn't willing to talk about it. What if she didn't want them? What if she wanted to leave? Damon knew he loved her enough already to let her go if that's what would make her happy, even if it meant he wouldn't survive it. Werewolves couldn't survive without their mates, so once bound together by the mating bond, if something happened to one, the other would die of a broken heart. He wouldn't tell her that, he decided. If she stayed, it wouldn't be out of guilt or obligation. He wanted her so much that he would die for her.

He had seen the pain behind her eyes, and knew that she hadn't had it easy. He wondered what had happened to her family, and why she didn't have any close friends. She was such a loving, gentle soul, that is until he and Devin walked into the room. Then she seemed to be on edge and snippy. Damon knew it was because she didn't understand the mating bond. She didn't understand her physical need to be close to them, and to touch them. She was probably fighting her own instincts, and that hurt him. If he could just explain the changes that were taking place in her body, maybe they could work this all out.

He sighed deeply. Right now he would just have to be happy holding his woman close to him while she slept. They would have to talk to her, and force her to understand, but he wouldn't wake her to do it. He drifted off to sleep with her breast in his hand, and her head on his bicep.

CHAPTER EIGHT

*C*aroline woke up in the bed tangled in male limbs again, and couldn't keep the groan from escaping her throat. *Damn it. How did I let this happen again? she thought. I was supposed to be leaving, storming out mad, and never looking back!*

Instead she was still naked under the soft bathrobe, which had now fallen completely open, and her nudity was pressed delightfully close to Damon's denim-covered cock. He was awake. She could feel his intake of breath, and his shaft was a huge bulge under her thigh. She ached to rub against it, and have him bring her back to orgasm with his touch.

Instead she rolled over, and sat up, drawing the robe closed with her. As she sat up, she saw Devin in the doorway with a lost look on his face. He leaned against the doorjamb with his hands in his pockets, and one ankle crossed over the other. The man who looked angry most of the time and spent all his time trying to control those around him, really just looked like he needed a hug now. She couldn't be angry with him. No matter how condescending and arrogant his need to claim her seemed.

"Caroline, are you okay?" he asked. His voice was a controlled

79

whisper, but the tenderness in it made her breath catch. There was worry in his words, but fear in his tone.

"Devin…" She paused. She couldn't bring herself to tell him she was leaving. In her heart she wondered if she would ever be able to leave him, no matter what. He was under her skin and in her veins now. She stood up and moved into his arms which opened up to her automatically. The feeling of his strong heartbeat against her cheek and his thick arms around her made her melt into him. "I'm okay, Devin. I'm sorry I got so upset. I'm independent, and I don't like being controlled and forced to accept decisions made for me. If that's what you need from a mate, then I'm not her. I can't be her."

Caroline stared at the wall while she made her statement of independence, because she was afraid it would make him walk away. Fear gripped her lungs for just a moment while he stood silent. She had just given him the excuse to send her packing, and she nervously waited for his response.

It came with a finger under her chin and a soft kiss on her pink lips. "Sugar, you're wrong, you are her. You are perfect for me. Even if you are a little bit headstrong. I wouldn't want you any other way. I need you to understand how this all works, but I didn't want to tell you everything last night. The last several days have been nothing but upheaval for you, so I wanted you to have some peace as we explained everything to you in little doses. I want you to trust me, and know that I would *never* make a decision for you that wasn't for your own good."

She could see his heart in his eyes, and the love in her chest swelled into a smile on her face. Relief rushed through her that he still wanted her.

"I can't promise not to argue with you, Devin."

"Good, don't make promises you can't keep." Damon spoke from behind her as he moved up against her back. She leaned backward just a bit to feel his warm strength against her, and her eyes closed as her skin tingled with desire at being trapped between the two deliciously sexy men. Her pussy dripped, and her nipples hardened, thinking about all the things these men made her feel in the last twenty-four hours.

"Caroline, look at me." Devin's voice rumbled into her now passion-filled, foggy brain, and her eyes cracked back open to peer at him. "As much as I want to bend you over right now and fuck you until you scream, we have to talk. We can't avoid this conversation."

"Please, Devin, fuck now, talk later," she demanded, rocking her hips up against Devin's erection, and then backward against Damon's. They both growled that sexy growl, and she heard a third growl that surprised her because it came from her own chest.

Damon chuckled under his breath. "Shit, that was so sexy. I can't wait until you growl with every moan, beautiful!" He turned her head to the side to meet his tongue in a hot kiss before she could respond. She felt him pull the robe from her body, leaving her naked to their touch.

Electricity crackled in the air, and Devin made a decision to join them instead of arguing. She could feel him kissing his way down her neck, stopping only at the wound where he had bitten her last night. On that he placed a soft kiss, and a hesitant lick. The feeling of his broad tongue on the supremely sensitive spot almost made her climax right there.

Devin swept her up into his arms, and, taking her to the bed, he put her up on her knees with her head resting on her arms. Her ass was wiggling in the air so that both men could see her wet cunt.

"First, you need a little punishment. I told you that you would have to talk to us when you were upset, and today you chose to run away instead of talking about it. *And* you locked your bedroom door to us." Even as he spoke the rough words, he comforted her by continuing to kiss her back and flanks. His lips pressed hot against her tailbone, and his hands swept gently across her skin. She turned her head and saw Damon's cheeky grin, and knew that whatever Devin had planned, it was going to be good for them all.

"Okay," she whispered. "So punish me."

She felt Devin's smile on her rump as he nipped at her sensitive skin, and then he pulled his hand back and brought it down in a smack on her soft flesh. She jumped, but the only sound from her was a gush of air leaving her lungs. He spanked the other ass cheek, leaving her flesh hot and tingly, and this time she moaned loudly.

"Well look at that, Dev, our pretty baby likes a little pain with her pleasure." Damon's voice came from in front of her, and Caroline lifted her face to meet his stiff dick bobbing next to her. She wrapped her fingers around it like an anchor as Devin spanked her again, and then once more.

"Please…" she begged.

"Please? What do you need, sugar?" Devin asked her playfully. His hand was rubbing all over her rounded backside, and his cock dripped pre-cum. He brought his hand down against her cheeks more firmly this time, and she whimpered.

"Please touch me. I need you." She stretched her neck out as she pulled Damon forward by his cock to reach him. He teased her for a moment, running his swollen length over her lips, and then let her engulf him. She started sucking his cock like never before, determined to bring him to the edge of passion.

Devin knew that she was new to this, but watching her suck Damon, while her ass winked at him was so fucking hot. She was in the position of submission, and his inner wolf took in the sight and relished it. She was so damn perfect for them. She was proving to be submissive, but erotically responsive in the bedroom, and feisty outside of the bedroom. She would definitely keep them on their toes. He couldn't wait to see her in full wolf form.

He slid his fingers up to her wetness, and stroked her right to the edge of orgasm. She was purring as she bobbed on Damon's cock and enjoyed Devin's finger fuck. He decided to push her further this time, and, covering his fingers in her cream, he slid a finger into her anus. She jumped at the new intrusion, but after a few strokes, she started pushing back against his finger. He slipped another finger into her and started stretching her ass to take his cock. He couldn't wait to feel her between them, completely full of hot dick and screaming her release. As she fucked back on his fingers, he coated his cock in her juices by shoving into her pussy unexpectedly. She gasped and almost choked on the cock in her throat as the sudden full feeling pushed her to orgasm. Her whole body trembled with the intensity of her climax, but she managed to stay on her knees somehow.

Damon smiled big at Devin as their eyes met over her. Silently Devin used his eyes to convey his intentions to Damon before moving. Then with a deep breath, Devin moved his fingers down to Caroline's sensitive clit, and strummed it as he pushed his shaft into her tight asshole. It stretched, and Caroline cried out at the burning sensation.

"Shhhh, hush, sugar. It will feel good in just a second, push back on me, and focus on my fingers pinching your clit." He kept talking to her to distract her from her discomfort until he could feel her accepting his cock completely. He paused, just enjoying the feeling of her tight ass muscles fluttering around him. If he wasn't careful, this would be over way too quickly. He could feel the way her asshole was clenching and unclenching around him, trying to pull him deeper or push him away, and it blurred his vision for a few seconds.

"Oh my God, Devin, that feels so good!" She was moaning and writhing so much now that she couldn't keep sucking Damon anymore.

Devin lifted her up against his chest as Damon slipped down underneath her. Devin's muscles were clenched with steely control as he was still sunk balls deep in her ass, trying not to move.

Caroline thought she would explode if Devin didn't move soon, and in her aroused state she wasn't really aware of Damon moving underneath her.

"Please!" she begged. "Move, damn it."

"Caroline, hush. You need to learn to control your desires. Be patient, and it will be so much better, sugar." Devin spoke with his lips against her shoulder, and his voice sent waves of fire down her spine and through her clit. He was massaging her breasts and pinching her nipples as he held her still for Damon to get settled. Then he lowered her down, impaling her on Damon's erection. She screamed at the completely full feeling of having two cocks pressed tightly into her.

Damon swallowed the end of her scream with a hot kiss that made her squirm harder, trying to get them to move. She pressed her breasts against Damon's chest and arched her back against Devin's, craving more. They started slowly, just rocking a little, and as her cries of passion increased, they moved faster and harder until they were fucking her. As one man moved out, the other pushed in and they quickly set a rhythm pushing her until her body broke through the ceiling of passion and she saw stars. She vaguely heard their simultaneous cries of release as she collapsed on top of Damon. Her body felt like jelly and she was more satisfied than she had ever been in her life.

Devin pulled away, and when he came back, he had a warm washcloth that he used to clean her up. A wave of embarrassment at this intimate touch made her clench her thighs, but he gently pulled them apart, smiling at her and shaking his head. Once Damon and Caroline were clean, Devin went to the bathroom, and she heard the shower start.

She lay there for several minutes just basking in her pleasure. She had never done anything so naughty in her life, but she felt so complete with both men filling her full. Even now, just moments after the most amazing orgasm of her life, she could feel desire in her belly. It made her anxious that a part of her wanted desperately to pull Damon against her again and keep him with her forever. She could feel Damon's fingers dancing up and down her spine. His touch drifted over the sensitive patches of skin that marred her ass cheeks and she turned to look at him with a hot blush on her cheeks.

"You shouldn't feel ashamed that you got pleasure from us, Caroline. It's natural, and it will only get better as your wolf gets stronger."

Damon groaned, and she heard him holding his breath as she processed his words.

"What do you mean *my* wolf?" she asked, rolling over to look him straight in the eyes.

"That's what I wanted to talk to you about, Caroline, before all of this." Devin gestured to their disheveled state as he came back in the room with just a towel around his waist. "Why don't you get dressed, and we can talk." He patted her ass as she crawled out of the bed and reached for her clothes, and then headed out of the bedroom again.

Damon followed his brother down the hallway with a cheeky smile over his shoulder on his way out the door. He called behind him, "Don't keep us waiting."

She finished pulling her clothes on, wondering which brother had gathered them and folded them neatly on top of the dresser. Then she went to the bathroom and tried to brush the tangles from her curly hair with her fingers. The woman she saw in the mirror was well loved, and happy. She was stunned to realize she was happy with these two men. She couldn't remember the last time she felt completely happy and carefree. She had a sense of belonging when they were with her, but she had a gut instinct that whatever they were going to tell her was going to hurt.

"Okay, so start talking. What exactly does being your mate mean?" she asked as she followed them into the great room again. She took a seat on the couch, and felt a quick flash of heat in her loins as she remembered this was how last night's activities had started. This time though Damon and Devin sat on either side of her with their bodies turned toward her, and neither touched her.

They seemed to be conversing through their eyes again, and it pissed her off.

"What are you two saying? I know somehow you are talking, but I don't understand it." Her head swiveled between the two men, waiting for their answer.

Open your mind to us, sugar, and you will understand, too.

Caroline's eyes were huge as she stared at Devin. His mouth hadn't moved, but she had heard him as clearly as if it had.

As mates we will be able to share each other's thoughts telepathically. You just have to listen for us, and if you try you can send your thoughts to us as well.

What the fuck?

Devin and Damon both started laughing at the words their mate sent to them with her first conscious and focused thoughts. Still laughing, Devin started explaining out loud.

"I know it seems a little overwhelming, but let me back up. When Damon rescued you from the fire, he was somehow able to smell your scent. Wolves have a particularly good sense of smell, and each individual—wolf or human—has their own specific scent. A wolf's mate will always have a particularly appetizing scent that is more attractive to him than anyone else's. Your scent is what first told Damon and me that you were our mate, and once we got close enough to know you, we both fell in love with you."

"You can't love me yet," she argued. Her head was slightly spinning already, as she grasped for the patience to understand everything he was telling her.

"Why not? You are in love with us." Damon said it so matter-of-factly that Caroline knew she couldn't argue.

"So we live happily ever after? Two wolf firemen and the human woman? How does that work, guys?"

"Not exactly. You see, once we mated...er...made love, the mating bond started to form. It's an invisible imprint on your heart that bonds you to each of us for life. Everything you feel will affect us, and vice versa. We will be able to sense you and your feelings from now on, and if something happens to a wolf's mate, the surviving wolf won't last long." Devin was trying to go slow, and he was hoping that she would read between the lines. He really didn't want to shock her with the words.

"Guess it's a good thing that we aren't all three wolves then." She laughed nervously, but she caught the look exchanged between the men. "Oh my God! Are you telling me that I'm a wolf, too? Did you turn me into one, or was I always one and just didn't know it?"

Damon pulled her against his chest, trying to calm her nerves as Devin kept explaining.

"You became a wolf the first time we mated, because we both claimed you. The bite marks on your shoulders. They will never go away, and they mark you as our mate. We aren't completely bonded yet, because you have yet to mark us with your own bite. You will do that when you are ready. After that no other wolf will dare to approach any of us, because they will see the marks and we will carry each other's scent."

It was crazy to think about. Surely she was crazy to even believe it. Her thoughts zipped around in her brain making her slightly dizzy. *I'm a wolf, and these are my wolf mates?*

"You guys did it without telling me first? Why? So that you would have some sort of sicko hold on me? Am I going to sprout fur now?" she asked sarcastically. She knew she was lashing out in fear at them, but she couldn't help it. This decision was something she had no choice in now, and she felt violated somehow. The idea that her men would make a choice so important for her, hurt her to the bone. She pushed Damon away from her, and stood up to pace the room.

"No, you won't just start sprouting fur. At the full moon, you will change, yes. For now you won't be able to stop it, but one day in the future you will have that kind of control. I'm sorry. We should have taken the time to explain more, but damn it, I wanted you so badly." Devin watched her patiently, as she put space between the three of them so that she could gather her thoughts. "We only have a few days until the full moon, and I would really like to present you to the pack as our mate."

"The pack?" She looked over her shoulder at him in confusion.

"Our family is called a pack—a wolf pack. We have a den—a home—just outside of the city. I am the Alpha of the pack, which basi-cally means I'm the leader. In the human world it would be the king. Damon, Liam, Owen, and Cash are some of my Betas or second-in-command. You will be an Alpha's mate, which in the human world is like a queen," Devin stated, and she spun around to stare at them.

"Queen? Me?" Her self-esteem issues clawed to the surface, and she felt her knees buckle. Damon was moving to catch her before she even knew she was falling. He sat in the chair with her in his arms, and stroked her hair from her face.

"Beautiful, don't doubt that you will make a great queen. You are compassionate and smart, and you already have the two most important pack members wrapped around your little finger." He smiled, and his dark-green eyes sparkled with love.

Leave it to Damon to make her feel better about something that scared her so much. Caroline couldn't stop turning the word *queen* over and over in her mind. She was just a regular person, a nurse at the local hospital, not a queen. There was nothing about her life that was even minutely royal. She couldn't pull it off, and the twins would regret choosing her as their mate.

"Not a chance, darlin'." Devin growled as he heard her thoughts. Her startled eyes looked straight into his, and she automatically held her arms out to him. She needed him to comfort her, too, so that she didn't start to panic at all this new information. And he was there. That fast he was on his knees in front of her with his head on her chest and his arms around her middle. Her heart swelled with emotion as Damon held her securely in his lap, and Devin embraced her, silently offering her the comfort and support that she needed.

Her world had just been flipped on its side, and she was struggling to get her feet back under her. She was in love with two men that she didn't really even know, and she was considering giving them her future. How would she explain this to her friends, and coworkers. The more she forced herself to look at the situation, the more her heart led her down this path. She knew that she had to follow this through and see where it took her. She wanted them to know that they hadn't scared her off, even if she was scared out of her mind.

"I love you, Devin, and you, too, Damon. Whatever happens, I love you guys. I don't know if I can do this, so don't start planning a wedding, but I'm not walking away. I need to know if this is real. I want to believe it is." She whispered it, but she needed to say it out loud.

They held her for what seemed like hours, but it was probably only minutes. It was Damon who broke the contact first, using his fingers to lift her chin until their eyes met.

"Hot damn, Dev. We've got ourselves a mate." His smile warmed her to her toes, and she couldn't help but return it. Grinning back, she turned to see Devin's reaction to his brother, and his beautiful face had burst into a radiant smile. She kept herself from restricting his statement, or playing the what-if game with herself. No matter what, she was just going to let this happen like it was intended, and enjoy every second she had with them.

"Come on. We are going out tonight, sugar. We need to talk with the boys more, and I definitely need to take you dancing." Devin pulled her up into his arms, and spun her around into a dip. This was a side of him she hadn't seen yet. Usually he was so serious, but this side of him was more like Damon, playful and happy. She couldn't hold her laughter in as he righted her and pulled her close. She looked up at them to find them smiling and staring at her again.

"What?" she said, laughing.

"You have to do that more often, beautiful. Your laugh is the sexiest sound I have ever heard in my life." Devin's words drove the sexual tension in the room high as she felt her stomach ball up with desire. "Oh, and your horny scent might get you fucked again instead of getting you to the store for clothes, so you better tame your thoughts."

Caroline smirked, and just to tease them a little, she deliberately pushed a few scandalously dirty thoughts their way.

Both men growled and then moaned as she sashayed off down the hallway to get her shoes.

She's going to be the death of us, Devin thought.

Yeah, but if I have to die, that's how I want to go. Damon couldn't wipe the smile from his face. He and Devin were mated now, and hopefully soon they would be starting a family. He was relieved that Caroline had taken their secret so well, but a mental image of her confusion and hesitation flitted through his brain. He was apprehensive that the conversation wasn't over yet. Shaking off his nerves, he followed his woman back down the hallway to get ready. He was determined to take her out and show her a good time.

CHAPTER NINE

*A*s they pulled into the gravel lot of a small country western bar, Caroline's stomach dropped to her knees, and she wondered for the millionth time how she possibly thought she was going to go out into public like this. When they left the house Devin and Damon had taken her directly to the mall to pick up more clothes. Devin pointedly ignored her arguments that she could pick out and purchase things for herself, and they spent the better part of an hour making a pile of bags and boxes from several upscale stores to restock her wardrobe. They picked out the expected dresses that were figure hugging, and heels and strappy sandals, along with sexy lingerie, and even a pair of delicate silver moon earrings that Damon caught her admiring. Then they surprised her by stopping in a Western-wear shop where they purchased skintight blue jeans, a button-down plaid shirt, a pair of lady's white cowboy boots, and a matching white cowboy hat. She had laughed at them and told them she wasn't country enough to wear boots and a hat, but they wouldn't listen.

"You ride as well as any cowgirl I've ever seen, beautiful!" Damon had argued, and she had given in reluctantly.

So here she was climbing out of Devin's huge pickup, looking like a rodeo queen, and feeling very out of place. The clothes were surprisingly comfortable, and well worth the arousing reaction that her appearance had on her men, but now she had to pull off the look in front of real cowboys? What was she thinking?

"Stop worrying, you look hot as hell," Damon said next to her ear as he helped her out of the truck. He moved her mahogany curls aside to kiss her neck, and she let out a nervous giggle.

"If you say so. So who all are we supposed to meet here?" she asked, looping her arm through Damon's and letting him pull her into the bar. Devin followed slightly behind them with a possessive hand on the small of her back. She loved knowing that she had him behind her, taking care of her.

It's just the guys from the firehouse, sugar. Relax.

Devin's words were a calming caress through her head, and she found herself smiling in spite of her nerves. They moved through the crowd quickly, and led her up onto a raised platform opposite the bar that was surrounded by a short railing. There were two round tables there with plush-looking circular booths wrapping around them. This was obviously the VIP section of the bar. Her eyes met those of Cash, Liam's, and Owen's, who tipped his beer bottle at her and looked distinctly more comfortable than he should have considering his clothing. He was still wearing dress clothes, but had lost the tie and jacket. He looked genuinely relaxed in this gritty environment, and she figured there must be more to him than she first assumed. Shaking off her curiosity at the enigma of Owen, she let her gaze sweep the rest of the occupants of the space.

There were two more men, and a couple of country-clothed bottle blondes snuggled cozily in the circle. The two women seemed to be quite happy seated in the middle of so much testosterone, and based on their glassy eyes, also seemed to be quite intoxicated.

Perfect, she thought to herself. *All I will have to chat with is sexy men that I'm not supposed to think are sexy because they are related to my boyfriends.*

She followed Damon into the booth and leaned into him as he settled back on the seat. Devin reached out and wrapped his arm around her shoulders as he sat next to her, and she smiled up at him. That was better. At least she knew that they wanted to be with her, and not the two bleach-blonde skanks across from them.

Damn, beautiful, chill out. Those two aren't my type. I promise you that you are so much hotter than they are, especially when you're riding my cock and screaming my name.

Caroline blushed at Damon, but couldn't help the gleeful feeling that settled over her as she realized she really was worrying about nothing. Her men wanted her, and no one else. Her confidence high, she leaned over to Liam who was closest to Damon.

"Hey guys, good to see you again! Looks like you're having fun." She smiled pointedly toward the bimbo on his arm, and he laughed gleefully.

"Good to see you, darlin', and we are always having fun! Did you lovebirds work out your issues today?" He grinned at Devin who shot him a black look. "Guess you don't want to talk about your feelings huh?"

"Fuck off, Gray," Devin said, and he ordered beers for the table. "Caroline, you know these three shits, but the two new ones are Rafe and Ryley Whetstone."

She smiled back at the two new faces taking them in and comparing them to her men. They had to be related as well, but she wasn't quite sure how they connected with Devin and Damon. Unlike the other five guys, these two looked like Norse Vikings. They both had yellow-gold hair and light-blue eyes. She guessed that Rafe was the oldest of the two because he had a few laugh lines around his mouth, and he kept his hair cut shorter. Ryley's hair was down to his shoulders and looked soft as silk. Their bodies were burly and even more muscular than her men, with thick necks and biceps that were probably bigger than her waist. She knew they were firemen because they both wore T-shirts emblazoned with the firehouse logo on them, but because of their laughing, light-blue eyes she wondered if they were wolves.

"The answer is yes, they are wolves, too, sugar," Devin answered, and she saw the two men in question smile wider, clearly knowing where her female mind had gone. "They are pack members, but not directly family. Although, I like to think of them as my brothers."

Rafe laughed out loud at this statement, "Hell yeah we're brothers, after everything we've suffered through with you, Devin!"

That got a loud laugh from everyone, and even Devin smiled.

"They are actually *my* foster brothers, though I don't admit that very often. I would hate to be lumped in with these soft pups." Liam's eyes sparkled with laughter as he teased the two blonde hunks. Ryley reached over the table to smack him in the back of the head which brought on another round of laughter. She decided she liked this rough and rowdy group of men, and she hoped she would like the rest of her new family as much.

"Okay, boys, clear the ladies out, we need to get our business over with so that I can relax." Devin indicated the two women seated with them, and his tone shut down any real argument from the men.

The two women however, looked disappointed and whined a bit as the guys moved to let them out of the booth. Eventually they wandered off to find someone else's arm to cling to. Caroline sat there nervously unsure of whether or not she was supposed to stay or go away, too, but Devin's arm remained tight around her shoulder, and Damon's hand on her upper thigh kept her seated.

"Tommie said that Barton is headed this way as we speak. He may already be here. Apparently Tommie's friend lost their trail just outside of the Des Moines city limits." Owen was looking at Devin, but speaking to the group. Caroline's brow furrowed as she tried to remember if someone had told her who Tommie was. And who was Barton?

"Damn. If he challenges me, I'll have to kill him. I can't leave him wounded to challenge me again later. This is not what I need right now." Devin ran a hand through his black hair in obvious frustration.

"What is he thinking? Why would he think that anyone in our pack would follow him as their leader? Most of his own pack doesn't even respect him as their Alpha!" Damon was clearly agitated.

It was Cash who leaned in closer and said, "Devin, we have the guys all on high alert, and if someone catches even a glimpse of his hide around here, we will know it. We can't wait for him to attack us. We need to be on the offense."

Caroline caught the glint of hunger for battle in his eyes, and looking around the table she could see the barely controlled rage and anxiety in each man. They were itching for a fight with this Barton guy.

"No, that's exactly what we are going to do. We are going to hold back and wait for his move. We all know that the other members of the Gray Pack will never accept Barton as their leader, but he is arrogant. He has hated me since we were kids and I showed him up in Memphis. His father gave him such a whooping that day that I even felt bad for him. If he wants a fight, he will have it, but I won't be accused of starting this war." Devin was restraining his own anger and trying to force a sense of calm on the group, but Caroline could feel it in his muscles. Whoever this Barton guy was, he was clearly a threat to him, and in turn to her.

"Who knows about Caroline?" Cash asked quietly. Caroline wasn't even sure she heard the question clearly over the music, but Damon's response cleared up her confusion.

"Only you guys know about our mate right now, but if Barton finds out, he will do everything in his power to use her against Devin. He will assume that she is his Achilles heel. We all know what happens to a wolf when their mate is taken from them. If he gets to her, the battle is over." There was an ominous silence as he paused and physically shook himself as if trying to clear the thoughts from his head before continuing. "We were planning to take her to the den this week over the full moon for her first change, so everyone else will find out then. I'm gonna need to call the chief because Dev and I need to be with her until Barton is found. We'll have to find coverage for our shifts at the station." Damon looked at Devin who silently nodded his agreement.

"Hold on a second. You guys are talking about me like I'm not here? Who is this Barton guy, and why would he give a rat's ass about me? I've never done anything to him. And why would you need to take time off of work to stay with me? I'm a big girl. In fact I've lived alone for the last decade and done just fine. I even know how to shoot a gun, and trust me I would shoot to kill." Caroline couldn't keep the irritation out of her voice. These men were acting like sexist apes. They weren't going to sit here and make decisions for her.

"Shit, why can't I find a good woman that can shoot?" Rafe grumbled.

"You'll be lucky if you can ever find any woman who will tolerate your cranky ass, bro, much less a good one." Ryley and the others laughed at his joke, but it was clear that they were all deadly serious about this situation.

"Caroline, Barton is an Alpha. His pack—the Diego Pack—is denned in Chicago. He is a power-hungry wolf who has decided he wants my pack to be his as well. I believe you when you say you think you can take care of yourself, but this isn't the average guy. You can't shoot him and do any real damage. He is a werewolf, and he has nothing to lose. He can, and will take advantage of my bond with you. I have no doubt. I want you protected, and that means having someone with you at all times." Devin's tone was bossy and controlling. Completely Alpha, was Caroline's first thought. She decided it would be better not to argue with him while they were out in public, but they would talk more about this at home.

"So we're all just going to go about our lives like there isn't a crazy wolf after us?" she asked incredulously. The other men wouldn't meet her eyes as she looked around the table. They were obviously going to follow Devin on this one.

"Yep, and I plan on dancing with my mate while my brother gets us some sustenance. Let's go!" Damon's smile was contagious as he pushed on her side. Devin moved out of the booth to let them up, and Damon took her cowboy hat off, dropping it in his bother's waiting hands. Then he pulled her toward the dance floor. Her irritation melted away as he spun her around into a quick dip before dropping a soft kiss on her lips. Then, grabbing her hand, he led her toward the dance floor.

She heard a long, low whistle behind her, and grinned back at Liam over her shoulder just to get under Devin's skin. All six males behind her had their eyes glued to her denim-covered ass as she walked away, and she couldn't resist the extra sway in her step just to twist the knife.

Behave, sugar, or I will spank your ass when we get home. Devin's voice in her head was husky with desire, so she shot back at him.

Promises, promises.

Damon swung her around into a slow dance as the loud music softened, and he pulled her close to him. Their foreheads met as he stared into her eyes. She could see the controlled heat in them as their bodies pressed together, and her now-hard nipples rubbed against his chest. She moaned softly when he pulled her arms up around his neck and slid his hands down into her back pockets to hold her ass. Everyone around them disappeared as they seemed to move together as one unit. They rocked together in perfect harmony for the length of the song, and into the second slow song. The cotton of her shirt seemed to rasp erotically against her breasts, and her fingers found a path of their own through the hair at the nape of his neck. He pressed his erection hard against her and pulled her pelvis to meet him. They went from dancing to swaying with their own grinding motions. His heated masculine scent seared her brain and brought her blood to a rapid boil.

Her knees wobbled as she grew hornier, and she couldn't resist rising up on her toes to kiss him softly. Her lips drifted across his, and her tongue darted out to lick the seam of his mouth. She let her kisses roam down his neck, and she licked his pulse point hotly.

"How long until we can get out of here, Damon?" she whispered into his mouth, and he growled low in his chest.

"Oh, beautiful, I'm ready to get you naked now, but we have to wait until after Cash's set. He sings tonight, and he should be going on stage here shortly. Besides, Dev and I promised you a good night out. I promise, we will get naked the second we get home." He pulled away from her reluctantly, and she could see the ridge his hard-on made in his jeans.

She looked down at her own nipples which stared back pointedly through her shirt. There was no hiding her need, so she lifted her chin, and proudly headed back to the table with him. He kept his arm wrapped tightly around her waist, and she let herself lean heavily against him. He looked down at her, meeting her eyes. His face gave away his desire as his nostrils flared at her damp scent, and she felt more confident in herself as a woman than she ever had in her life. She intended to keep these two turned-on, so that they would get her home and screw her as hard as possible. She wanted them to forget their stresses and focus on how good they could feel with her. She felt like a whole person when they were holding her.

They reached the table and quickly took their seats as a waitress served the dinner that Devin had ordered for them. The waitress brought fresh beer, multiple plates with huge cheeseburgers, and baskets full of French fries. She watched as the men all dug into the food and couldn't hold back a laugh.

"What?" Liam asked.

"You guys sure eat like animals!" She was now laughing hard, and they all started laughing with her as they looked around the table. Seven men, one woman, fourteen cheeseburgers, and seven baskets of fries surrounded them. "How do you ever afford groceries?"

"Usually we are fairly satisfied after the full moon because we can hunt, but the few days leading up to it we are always hungry. For everything," Damon answered her, with a tempting wiggle of his eyebrows to indicate his meaning with his last statement.

Caroline blushed as the other men all agreed. She was truly enjoying herself, surrounded by these guys who laughed and joked with each other. They were close, and for a just a moment she envied their sense of family. Damon sensed her slight withdrawal and pulled her closer to him to whisper in her ear.

"They are your family, too, Caroline. Trust them, and they will protect you just like Dev and I. You are their Alpha's mate, and they will show you that respect, but they also want to be your friend." She met his gaze, and he brushed a quick kiss over her lips.

As usual it was the perfect thing to say to make her feel better. She relaxed into his arms, and listened to the group chat. No one brought up Tommie, or Barton, or the impending challenge and danger again, so Caroline wondered if she had overreacted a bit at the conversation. Clearly they weren't all that concerned about it, so she wouldn't be either. She would just cherish this moment with her new family.

Cash got up a few minutes later and left the table, so that he could prepare for his set on stage. Caroline watched as he and his band took the stage. He walked with a cocky swagger, and smiled with such charm that she could see he could have a seriously successful music career without ever singing. She wondered why he would choose to be a fireman when he controlled a crowd with just a look, and then when he started to sing, she was floored. He was amazing! His voice was deep and husky as it rumbled over the crowd, sending women into quivers of desire, and setting men to rocking in their boots. The people loved him, and Caroline found herself bouncing in her chair to the music.

She was surprised when Devin gripped her hand and pulled her from her seat so that he could lead her out to the dance floor. She had never line danced in her life, but she was swept up in the enthusiastic crowd and learned the steps quickly. She laughed and danced until her feet hurt, and sweat glistened on her brow. Devin, too, was laughing and grinning at her as he watched her dance.

"Damn, sugar, you didn't tell us you were a country girl at heart. I love watching you move." His tone was intimate and filled with heat as he watched her dance. She couldn't resist adding a little more shimmy to her moves, knowing that he was watching her and getting turned on.

When he finally led her back to the booth, Cash had just ended his set and swaggered offstage. Just before they took their seats, Devin pulled her against him and kissed her with more passion than she had ever felt from him. She knew the other men watched them, and she decided she didn't care. She tangled her fingers in his hair and held him close while they kissed. He stroked her tongue and swept his own into every part of her mouth. He nibbled her lips, and Caroline thought she was going to burst into flames.

"I think I'm going to need a fireman, babe, someone who can help me put out my fire." She whispered the words, but the other guys at the table cracked up as their keen wolf sense of hearing caught what she said.

"Damon, let's go," Devin demanded, and he winked at her before he turned back to the table full of men. "We'll see you boys later at the den."

With that he spun on his heels and tugged Caroline along with him as they left the bar for his truck. Caroline's clit was humming, and her throat was tight. She needed to come so bad that she reached out and grabbed Damon as they all settled into the front seat of the truck. She was between the two men, and logically she knew that the truck wasn't the best place to fuck, but she was out of her mind with need. The kiss she gave Damon was mind-blowing, and pushed her over the edge of reason.

Damon kissed her back, wiping all doubts from her mind as he helped her move over to straddle his lap. Caroline could hear Devin's growl as he watched the two of them making out next to him. She basked in their desire, they were as horny for her as she was for them.

Knowing Devin watched her turned her on, and she pushed her jeans and panties off of her legs. She moved over Damon, and pulled his cock from his jeans. He was hard as a post and dripped pre-cum all over her hand. She didn't hesitate to impale herself on him, and he groaned loudly.

"Fuck, beautiful! You are so wet and hot, and you feel so damn good. Slow down or this will be over too fast!" She preened at his words, and threw her head back so that he could kiss along her neck and breasts as she rode him like an expert cowgirl. Her thighs gripped his hips tightly, and her Kegel muscles milked his cock. He pounded into her, triggering her to scream out an orgasm as he bit her hard nipple. As the wave of passion swamped her, he let go and released his seed into her womb. She collapsed against him, gasping at the intensity of the orgasm, and trying to get her head to quit spinning.

She looked over at Devin who drove, stoically looking at the road. He looked so tense that she almost giggled. He must have enjoyed the show judging by the bulge under his zipper. Before she could question herself, she moved off of Damon, and crouched on the seat with her head next to Devin's lap. She reached out and unzipped his mammoth rod, wrapping her fingers around him tightly. She was turned on to see that her fingers didn't quite meet around his thickness.

"Wow, sugar, what are you doing? We're almost home, and I have to get us there in one piece." She could hear his words, but she didn't care what he said. She knew what she wanted, and she wouldn't stop until she had it. She wanted her Alpha wolf to lose control. She needed him to let go of control and want her as much as she wanted him.

She ran her tongue around his red, throbbing cock head, and licked from his balls to the crown, tasting his seed. He was smoky and salty, and made her hotter than hell. She pulled him deep into her mouth, and started bobbing up and down on his cock. Her tongue tickled the spot where his crown met his shaft every time she pulled back, and he hit the back of her tonsils every time she pushed forward. He was groaning, and desperately trying to get them home quickly.

Caroline could feel Damon's hands on her naked ass, and her dripping cunt as she worked Devin's hard-on over. She pushed back against his fingers, and he stroked her from clit to anus, and back. Devin wrapped one hand in her loose hair after tossing her new hat to the floor, and forced her to swallow him deeper.

She focused on breathing through her nose, and she felt his length slip a little farther down her throat. Pleased with his growl, she did it again. She ran her hand between his legs and squeezed his balls. It was just enough to push him over the edge, and he pumped her mouth full of cum. She swallowed every drop and licked him clean. Then she sat up and grinned at him.

"Sugar, if that's the reward we get for taking you out, then prepare to have an active social life." His breathing was rough and fast as he struggled to park the truck in their driveway. After pulling the keys from the ignition, he grabbed her by the back of her neck and pulled her against him to kiss her deeply. "Now get your sexy ass in the house. I need to fuck you."

She laughed, and jerking her jeans up her legs, she jumped out of the truck, grateful that Damon kept his hands at her hips to steady her. Her legs were shaking she was so turned on, and she wasn't sure she could walk all the way to the bedroom. Damon must have sensed her hesitation because he swung her up into his arms, and smiled possessively as she put both arms around his neck. He carried her up to the house behind Devin, but they were all stopped dead in their tracks at the sight that greeted them when he opened the door.

CHAPTER TEN

The house had been ransacked, and it looked like absolutely nothing had been left untouched. The kitchen cabinets were emptied all over the counters and floors, and they stood open. Packages of food had been ripped open and left scattered. The poker table lay on its side with one leg broken, and even the couch cushions had been ripped open. The large screen TV lay facedown on the floor, and the pieces of plastic around it indicated that it had probably been intentionally broken. The curtains hung in a torn jumble from a broken curtain rod, and the mirror directly in front of the front door had been smashed. It held the distinct imprint of a fist amidst the spiderweb of cracked glass. She smelled a musty, sour smell that was so overpowering she felt the urge to retch.

Damon set her down on her feet and pushed her behind him as Devin put his fingers to his lips to keep them quiet. The two men moved silently throughout the house, checking that no one was still in it. She couldn't hear even the whisper of movement as they checked every crevice of the house for lurking intruders. Once they were assured the house was empty, they regrouped in the doorway where

Caroline stood stunned. She wanted to cry, or scream, or something, but all she could do was stare blankly at the disaster around her.

"Come on, Caroline, let's go back outside." Damon's voice wasn't much louder than a whisper as he hugged her tightly and then nudged her back out the door to sit on the pretty iron bench on the porch.

Devin pulled his cell phone from his back pocket and paced back and forth on the lawn while he talked. She heard him tell someone what they had just found, and after a short three-part conversation between him, the person he called, and Damon, the two men led her back to the waiting truck where Damon buckled her into the passenger seat. He placed her forgotten hat on her head, and gently kissed her lips.

"Devin is going to take you away from here, and I'm going to wait for the guys. We're going to find out what happened and clean up the mess before we bring you back here. I wish I could go with you to introduce you to the rest of the pack, but I need to stay here. I love you, Caroline." Her shock became even more defined as she whispered back to him.

"I love you, Damon. Stay safe, and hurry your ass up. I want you with me." He grinned at her and shut her door. Then he watched them leave with a brief wave.

They drove in silence for about fifteen minutes as Caroline tried to swallow her shock and think clearly again.

"Devin, who would do that to your house?" she asked, watching his face for his reaction to her question.

"Barton Diego," he said.

"How do you know it was him?" she responded, watching his reaction closely.

"The smell. His scent was all over the room, and he wanted us to know he had been there." His jaw clenched and unclenched with barely contained rage.

"But *why?*"

"He probably showed up at the house looking for me, and when I wasn't there, he got pissed." He paused and looked over at her. "Sugar, don't freak out, but now he knows about you. Our mating scent is all over that house, and he will make the connection and know I have found my mate. I believe he will come after you and try to find a way to use you to weaken me before he challenges me."

"Stupid man. Doesn't he know you don't fuck with an Alpha's mate?" She smiled shakily at him, and he smiled a much more relaxed smile back at her response. He reached over and grabbed her knee to pull her across the seat to him.

"Come here, sugar. I need you close." She snuggled under his arm, and inhaled his smoky cedar scent.

After a few more moments she asked, "So where are we going, Devin?"

"Home, Caroline. We are going to the pack den, where I know you will be safe." He didn't look at her as he spoke, and she felt her nerves tighten in her belly into a ball.

They were going to the den, which meant she was going to have to meet his entire family, and she would be surrounded by werewolves. *Oh my god, this night started out so good. I can't believe it could turn out so screwed up.* Her thoughts were jumbled, and her nerves were growing.

They were outside of Kansas City now, and the dark outside the windows was oppressive as she considered how his family would react to a woman he had only known for days. What if they hated her?

They won't hate you, beautiful. They will love you because we love you, trust us.

Damon's words warmed her. He always seems to know what to say to calm my nerves, Caroline thought and relaxed back into the seat cuddled under Devin's strong arm.

Devin smiled at his twin's input. The mating bond was growing quickly if Caroline could hear Damon from this distance, and that pleased him immensely. He needed her like he needed air in his lungs, and soon he hoped she would be ready to claim them like they had claimed her.

He kept her pressed against him for her sake, as well as his own. Seeing his house torn apart didn't scare him, but it sure as hell pissed him off. He had to bite the inside of his cheek to keep his wolf under control. Him changing into a pissed-off wolf in front of Caroline when she was in so much shock already wouldn't be a great idea.

He knew that Damon and his cousins would take care of the house, but he had no idea how they were going to find Barton. He hated waiting for bad things to happen. He was usually focused on preventing bad things from happening if he could, but this fight was inevitable. Barton had threatened Devin's status multiple times in words and actions, and now it seemed he finally had balls enough to challenge him properly. Devin had no fear of losing to the wolf, but he was scared for Caroline. If something went wrong and Barton got to her, or if something happened to him…he couldn't bear to think what the result would be.

Devin thought back to when he was a kid in Memphis at the Eastern US Pack School. His father had forced both him and Damon to go to school for the required two years to learn the standard pack etiquette of Alpha males. Damon had resisted loudly, complaining that he didn't need schooling when he had Devin around to be the Alpha of the pack. His father had insisted, just in case anything was to happen to Devin, it would be up to Damon to fill his shoes.

They were educated on everything from how pack law was created and worked, to how each of the eight individual packs in the United States had come into existence. Werewolves had been around for thousands of years, but they still kept their true forms secret from humans. To announce to a human that they had a wolf living next door to them usually brought about a terrible result, so it was easier to just keep their true selves secret.

They were taught about packs that existed in other countries, and had even had an exchange program for wolves who wanted to branch out and see the world. Outside of their animalistic tendencies it was exactly what you might expect from a secondary education boarding school. Devin and Damon had made lasting friendships with members of the various packs around the country. Unfortunately, only one particular pack stood out as refusing to be a part of the standard culture of the wolf community. The Diego Pack had long been the outcast of the eight wolf packs that dotted the United States, and there were plenty of rumors of violence and debauchery on behalf of them.

The feud between Barton Diego, who was heir to the Diego Pack, and himself had started in Memphis, although Devin really couldn't pinpoint exactly when our how it started. There was always plenty of competition between the two Alpha males as well as a lot of trash talking. Devin was quick to interfere when Barton started bullying someone, and Barton chafed at the interference. Their rivalry culminated on their graduation day when Devin was elected Supreme Alpha of their class by a majority vote, and Barton was the runner up.

Barton had relished telling his peers about his lineage and that his own father, and grandfather had both been voted Supreme Alpha during their years at pack school. Unfortunately for Barton, he was extremely arrogant, and his selfish ways grated on his fellow students' nerves. Devin had always been a strong leader at the school, he excelled in sports, made friends easily, and he was one of the top students in his studies. Barton took it personally when Devin beat him at this one contest. Barton had believed that he had the contest won already, and Devin topping him drove him crazy.

More recently there had been several wolves that had defected from the Diego pack, and joined the Gray pack. Devin had given much thought to the problems that it could cause if he took on members from his old nemesis's pack, but after hearing some of the cruel bullying tactics that Barton was using, he acquiesced. One young female wolf had reached them, bloody and broken, after escaping an attempted rape by Barton's beta wolf, Rolando. She had told them that Barton encouraged his beta to find a female he wanted, and not stop until she was well mated. Her tale of Barton drinking beer with the other male wolves while she was in the next room being viciously beaten boiled Devin's blood. He looked forward to sinking his fangs into Barton's tough hide and avenging her.

This would likely be a fight to the death because the alternative was unbearable. Worst-case scenario, he lost and wasn't killed, so he had to watch a mutt like Barton take over his pack, but he couldn't think that way right now. He had to focus on Caroline, and introducing her to his family would definitely take his mind off of the dangers surrounding them.

He held her close, enjoying the skittering of his flesh as her fingers drew patterns on his upper thigh. She seemed to be lost in her own thoughts, and Devin didn't want to invade her privacy so he resisted the urge to listen in. She was so warm, and welcoming to his friends. He loved how accepting she was of them, and how easily she seemed to be fitting into their lives. He prayed that she would be just as loving and accepting with the rest of his pack. The pack would accept her because of what she was to him, but he wouldn't be able to find peace if she didn't accept them and their culture.

No matter how much love he saw in her eyes, he couldn't help but see the fear and sadness, too. She was still reeling from all the trauma she had faced in the last few days, and he was afraid when the dust settled, she would turn tail and run. Shaking off his feelings of dread, he redirected his thoughts to what was happening in town.

What did you guys find, Damon?

Ryley and Liam are following the scent trail, and Owen is going over the house with Cash looking for any clues that will tell us this was Barton, but I don't need more evidence. We all smelled him here. I know that's who it was, Devin.

I'm in full agreement. Were you able to figure out what they were searching for?

Not yet, but there has been too much happening to go over the house with a fine-tooth comb for evidence. Once the police have taken the report, me and the guys will check it over top to bottom. I have to wonder if it was more for intimidation.

The attack and search of the house were both very personal. He wanted me to know he was in my house and that I was vulnerable.

No shit, did you see what they did to Caroline's room?

~

Caroline couldn't resist interjecting now, she had tried to keep quiet so that they wouldn't know she was listening and she could learn more information.

What did they do to my room, Damon?

Shit. The brothers both groaned the same groan even though they were miles apart.

Tell me, Damon, please? I hate that you are hiding something from me.

No, beautiful. I'm not hiding anything, but I do want to protect you.

I need to know what we are facing, too. The delayed response told her how much he regretted having to share any of the details with her.

They tore your room up pretty bad, worse than the great room. The quilt was in tatters, and the chest of drawers was purposely broken into pieces. He paused, but sensing there was more, she prodded him.

And?

The bathrobe I bought for you was spread out over the bed with a knife stabbed into it, and they left a message on the wall for us. Devin growled at Damon's words, and tightened his hold on Caroline as they drove. She stared at him wide-eyed waiting for Damon to finish.

What was the message Damon?

Caroline…

No, I need to know. What was the message?

"She dies first."

Caroline couldn't stop the gasp she let out any more than she could control the angry rage that settled over her. This fucker was threatening her and her men, and she would be damned if she was going to just sit back and let him.

Don't worry, sugar, he's just trying to scare us. Trust me, Damon and I will protect you with our lives. I will issue a legitimate challenge to him after we get to the den and talk it over with the rest of the pack. I already know I have the boys' support. Once you have searched the house, I want you all to head for the den, so that we can have a pack meeting to introduce Caroline.

Dev, are you sure we shouldn't delay her introduction until after Barton is dealt with? Damon sounded skeptical about a celebration, and Caroline couldn't stop the stab of pain in her chest. Was he trying to keep an opening to get out of this relationship if things didn't work out as planned?

No. We must acknowledge the mating bond immediately. You know as well as I do that a wolf is stronger with its mate beside him.

All right. We'll be there as fast as we can. I have to go talk with the police now that they finally got their asses here to take the report. Take care of our mate, Dev.

I love you, Damon. Caroline had to grit her teeth to keep from asking him to come to her. He was where he needed to be, and Devin was taking care of her. She couldn't make him choose.

Love you, too, beautiful!

Devin, and Caroline both sat in silence, absorbed in their thoughts for several minutes after Damon's last statement.

"If you challenge him, he has to fight you, right? He can't back down from it?" she asked Devin bluntly. She needed answers so that she knew what they were facing.

"Yes."

"To the death?" she pushed him, and she could see he didn't want to answer.

"Yes. This fight can only end in death." His jaw clenched, and she could see the muscles jumping.

"Will you win?" she whispered.

"Yes." His response was arrogant and cocky, but she believed that he believed it. She didn't respond to him, but continued to watch him. He swallowed hard, and she could see his Adam's apple bob in his throat.

"Stop doubting me, sugar. Barton doesn't understand that I have a secret weapon that he couldn't hope to find. I have you to live for, and I will fight with everything I have to make sure I can spend the rest of my life with you."

He brought her hand up to his lips and kissed it softly. She moved to stroke his hair back from his face, and she watched him as he watched the road. A momentary flare of panic at his words of forever hit her gut, and she forced it back down. Devin didn't need to be worried about her commitment issues right now.

"Good. So when do we get home? I'm exhausted." She yawned and stretched, and he laughed. The mood considerably lighter, he answered her.

"Right up ahead, sugar. You should start seeing wolves shortly. The pack owns the land we are on right now. Actually, we own about 500 acres of land around here and farther west. That gives us plenty of room to run and enjoy our wolf forms when we feel the urge."

"How many wolves are in the pack, Devin?" She was curious at how large her *new* family would be.

"About ninety of us right now, but we have a couple of females pregnant, and we just accepted a few new members recently."

"Wow! Are there wolf packs everywhere?" He grinned at her as she questioned him. Her body was lit with nervous excitement as she tried to put all of this new information together in her head.

"There are only seven packs in the lower forty-eight states of the US, and another one up in Alaska. There are several other packs around the world though. We are one of the largest and oldest wolf packs. Now, watch out the window, and you should be able to pick up movement soon." He pointed out the front window indicating the soft glow of the truck's headlights. She twisted back around to face out the windows into the black night. How did he possibly think she would see anything in the dark? And then she saw.

She could see dark shapes moving through the trees on both sides of her. They had turned onto a gravel road that was leading deeper into the woods, and as the shapes moved closer to her, she could see clearly they were wolves. Their eyes flashed in the headlights, and they seemed to be keeping pace with the truck, just following them.

They rounded a corner, and sitting before Caroline was the most beautiful log cabin she had ever seen. It was enormous, and it had huge solid-glass windows running the length of the front porch which wrapped around the side of the building. There were wolves all over the porch, and coming out of the front door of the cabin as well.

She took a deep breath, and, gripping Devin's hand tightly, they got out of the truck. A large black wolf moved swiftly toward them, and she watched as it change into a tall, lanky man with the same chocolate-brown hair covering his head and chest. She felt the blush on her cheeks as she looked away from his nudity. Obviously they were much more comfortable with being naked around here than she was. That would take some getting used to.

He stepped up to hug Devin, and then turned to her. After a quick once-over he wrapped her into a hug as well.

"Welcome, daughter!" he said loudly as he pulled back to look into her eyes. He had warm, friendly green eyes that took her in and immediately made her forget that he was completely naked. She felt welcome, and she smiled back at Devin's father.

"Thank you, sir."

"Aww hell, I'm Jim to you, sweetie. We don't call anyone *sir* around here!" He wrapped one arm around her shoulders and turned her to meet a small woman with dark-bronze skin and midnight-black hair. Thankfully she was wearing clothing. Caroline knew before introduction who the woman was, and she smiled at her warmly.

"Welcome, Caroline. I'm Sienna, Devin and Damon's mother. I'm so happy to finally meet you." She placed her hand on Caroline's jaw, and kissed her softly on the cheek. Caroline felt tears burning her eyes at the easy way these two accepted her and seemed to love her without question. "Don't mind my Jim, dear. He hasn't ever been human so he doesn't understand the modesty issues they have."

"Thank you, I'm happy to meet you, too," she responded automatically to the openness of the greeting. Her brows lifted at the indication that Sienna might understand being a human. She would have to ask Devin more about that later.

I told you they would love you, beautiful.

Hush, Damon. I need to get to know your family now. Come home soon, I miss you.

Yeah, I miss you, too. I can't wait to get you up on your knees so that I can show you how much.

She could hear the laughter in his voice as her pulse sped up at his words. It had only been about two hours since she had had him in the truck, but she craved his touch already. She wished desperately she could find a way to sneak out with Devin to scratch the itch between her thighs. Based on the number of werewolves surrounding them as they moved into the cabin, it wasn't looking like it would happen soon.

"Come now, Caroline. I have a feeling that you are tired and would probably like a bath and your bed. Most of the pack is in this yard just to catch a quick glimpse of you, but we can do introductions tomorrow. Let me show you to Devin's room so that you can rest, and we will talk more in the morning when you are refreshed." Sienna had one arm looped through Caroline's, and the other around Devin's trim waist. Devin had wrapped his arm around his mother's shoulders, and even though he had to stoop to reach the small woman, he kissed the top of her head.

"Thank you for understanding, Mama. My mate has been through a lot in the last few days, and faces much more in the next several." His relieved voice echoed in Caroline's ears, and she sighed her own pleasure at the promise of a soft bed.

"I have no doubt she has been through the ringer with my boys as her mates." Sienna winked at Caroline, and they both laughed. Caroline couldn't help the soft blush that rose on her cheeks at the double meaning in his mother's words.

"Not exactly what I meant." He had the good graces to look slightly shamefaced before he kissed Caroline gently and nudged her to follow his mother. "Go with Mama, sugar, and I will be up shortly."

Sienna led Caroline up a grand log staircase to a landing, and Caroline couldn't help but gape at the view of the great room from above. The landing at the top of the stairs was a loft that held a pool table, a foosball table and several pub tables with bar stools. A large TV hugged one wall and faced a comfortable-looking couch. There were two separate hallways leading off of the landing in either direction, and she could see that there were multiple doors off of each hallway. She wondered if all those doors were bedrooms. Hanging high over the two-story great room was a large chandelier that was simple but elegant, and held at least one hundred lights. The massive windows that wrapped the front of the house reflected back the light, making the huge space seem cozy somehow. This cabin was bigger than any home she had ever been in, and it was overwhelming.

Caroline must have looked a bit overwhelmed as she took it all in, because Sienna gripped her hand tighter and said, "This is our home, Caroline, and I know it seems like a lot all at once, but I hope you feel welcome here. I have dreamed of the day that my boys would take a mate, and I'm so happy to have you here."

"Thank you, Sienna. I love the guys so much, but I haven't agreed to forever with them. I told them I needed a little more time to think everything through. I'm not sure how much more I can take. I have had so many things change in my life in the last forty-eight hours, and I feel like it's all been a dream. Like tomorrow when I wake up I will still be in my little apartment, and I will have overslept and be late for my shift at the hospital." They laughed together as Sienna led her down one of the hallways to the very last door, and stopped.

"It's not a dream, dear, and I for one am glad. Whether or not you have accepted their offer of forever will not change the fate you are destined for. A wolf knows its mate by the link they share in their soul. I am glad to hear that my boys are smart enough to allow you time to adjust to this new life. Now, let's get you settled in for tonight so that you can rest, and we will talk more in the morning." She opened the door to a massive bedroom, and ushered Caroline in. She rushed through the room and turned on a gas fireplace that was at the foot of the king-size bed. "Brr...It's chilly up here. No one uses Devin's room when he's not here, so we have kept it closed up until today. There are clean sheets on the bed, and fresh towels in the bathroom. I expect he will be up shortly with a change of clothes for you. Would you like anything else? A cup of tea before bed perhaps?"

"Oh, thank you, but no. I think I will just take a quick shower and go to bed. I'm really exhausted." She stood awkwardly as Sienna smiled at her, and then Sienna pulled her into her small arms and gave her a loving hug. Caroline gripped her back tightly and clenched her eyes shut against the sting of tears. She couldn't imagine a more perfect mother-in-law.

As Sienna pulled back, she kissed Caroline on the cheek softly and said "All right, good night, dear." And then she hustled out of the room closing the door behind her.

Caroline spun around in a circle throwing her arms out with a huge smile and laugh. What a wonderful welcome to this new life. She stood for a moment in front of the heat of the fireplace, and then took to exploring her new room. The bed was enormous, and was covered in another lovely handmade quilt that was made up of tiny diamond-shaped pieces of fabric. She ran her hand over the stitching, wondering how many hours the piece had taken, and who might have put so much love into it. There was a sitting area by the bay window that had a small loveseat and a wingback chair in it, and she could see a bookshelf tucked in a corner that held an array of hardback books. She would definitely have to explore that later, she assured herself.

She drifted into the bathroom. It was masculine, all metal and stone, angles and hard lines. It had granite counters, an enormous open shower with multiple showerheads, and a free-standing soaking tub. All thoughts of a quick shower flew out of her mind when she laid eyes on that tub, and she instantly started the water running to fill it up. She found some soap, shampoo, and conditioner in the cabinet under the sink, and she stripped her clothes off to settle in for a long soak.

As she lay in the tub, her thoughts jumped all over the place. She wondered what Devin and Damon were doing. This tub was enormous, and they could probably all three fit. She shivered at the heat that idea caused in her loins. She let her mind wander over her feelings for them.

They fit her so well, and she was so comfortable with them. Like a well-worn pair of jeans, they molded to her, and she wondered if she actually fit them just as well. She knew that they had told her they wanted to keep her forever, but what did forever really mean? She had a job, and bills, and responsibilities. This fantasy had been amazing, and she wanted so badly to continue on living a carefree existence made of loving her men and nothing else, but she didn't push herself through nursing school just to walk away from it. She was a damn good nurse, and she knew it, so if the twins thought she was going to just give up herself to be their mate, they were way off base.

She needed to talk to them, but she was scared of what their answers would be. They were so affectionate and caring that it blew her mind. She had never felt so feminine with any other man, and they were intent on taking care of her. While she appreciated their protective nature, she was afraid that they might want her to be more submissive and fragile to appease their ego. That's how her last boyfriend had been. He wanted her to simper and praise him all the time. There was no way she was going to just let a man lead her around by her nose like that again. She had a backbone, and more confidence now than she had had right after her parents died.

Her success at work had brought her a peace in her life, and she looked forward to the challenges of her job. As a nurse in the emergency room, her shifts were chaotic at best, and the adrenaline of a fast-paced environment drove her. How would she shut all that off if they asked her to live here with them at the den? As much as she loved meeting his family, and enjoyed the luxurious cabin, she just wasn't willing to sit around waiting for them to tell her what to do every day. If they wanted her, then they would have to accept her as she was. End of story.

Devin stood in the doorway of the bathroom, watching her soak in the tub and listening as her mind wandered. He wanted to reassure her, but he wasn't sure of anything himself. He wanted to wrap her in his arms and make promises that they would be together forever, and she could maintain her old life, too. He knew that he would do anything in his power to ensure her happiness, but first he had to ensure her safety. She didn't seem to take the danger facing them very seriously, but he didn't know if he wanted her to. He couldn't stand to see her scared, and smell her fear.

Were they doing the right thing? Maybe they should have let her walk away yesterday? Immediately his wolf leapt to the surface in full battle mode. He knew that there was no possibility of walking away from his mate. He was in it for the long haul, and he would just have to help her believe in forever. He loved her spunk and vigor, and enjoyed matching wits with her.

"Need any help?" he asked her quietly.

She didn't even flinch at his voice. He wondered if she somehow sensed his presence there, but he didn't question her.

"Actually, the water is getting cold, so I need to get out. Can you hand me a towel?" She slowly stood up and watched his reaction to her as the water sluiced off of her naked body into the tub. He swallowed hard, and held the towel out so that she could wrap into it. Goose bumps popped up on her flesh as he kissed her neck and shoulder, and then took to rubbing her dry with the towel. When she was completely dry, he picked her up and carried her to the bed without a word. He tucked her under the covers with a kiss on the nose, and smiled at her.

"Sugar, you go on to sleep. As much as I want to crawl in there with you, you need some serious rest, and I need a shower. I'll be back in a few minutes. I love you." He whispered the last few words to her as her eyes drifted shut, and she fell into a deep, restful sleep. She never even noticed when he returned to join her in the bed a little while later and pulled her sleeping form tight against his body. He cradled her close, burying his nose into her hair, and slept.

CHAPTER ELEVEN

*W*hen Caroline woke the next morning, the sun was barely up, and she could feel Devin's steady breathing against her ear. She was spooned against his hard length, and buried under the heavy quilt. The fire was off, and she could hear birds chirping just outside the bay window. As she rubbed the sleep from her eyes, she unconsciously pressed her ass back against Devin's groin, and his cock hardened behind her. She heard his groan as he pressed forward, meeting her already sopping-wet pussy. He pressed into her, and they both paused to just enjoy the sensation of their connection. He thrust softly for a few moments, and then pulled from her, ignoring her grumble of dismay. He flipped her onto her back, and covered her small body with his own until he was bracing himself over her, resting on his forearms on either side of her head. The position pressed her breasts tightly to his chest, and made her feel protected and delicate. She twisted back and forth, pressing against him as the pressure to orgasm built within her. He thrust back into her slowly, and she moaned, sucking in a deep breath of air as her eyes drifted back closed.

"Open your eyes, sugar. Look at me, and know it's me." Their gazes collided, and Caroline almost came just seeing the passion in his eyes. His gaze warmed her soul and made her body tremble harder. Goose bumps rose on her skin and she could feel her heart racing.

As he began to move, he shifted to one arm and with the other caressed her body from her knee to the top of her head, touching her skin, kneading her muscles, and tweaking her nipples. He made love to her slowly, putting every ounce of feeling he had in his heart into his body. This was nothing like the wild, passionate sex of the last few days. Instead Caroline found herself slowly climbing a mountain of passion, and at the peak she felt herself jump off into oblivion.

"Not yet, sugar. Don't come yet." His words took a moment to sink into her brain as he slowed his thrusts to almost a standstill, letting her pull back from her impending climax.

"Please, Devin. Please, I need to come." She begged him.

"I want to come inside of you at the same time as your climax rolls through your sweet pussy. Let the anticipation build." He continued his steady movements, but added a delightful little hip roll when he plunged deep inside of her. Each time he rocked his cock into her soft valley, the tight pressure in her belly grew. She writhed on the bed underneath him, reaching out to grab whatever happened to be close. This resulted in her hands gripping his enormous biceps until her fingernails drew blood.

"Yes, please, Devin. Now!" She dug her heels into the bed and arched her whole body like a tightly plucked violin string.

He let his weight press down onto her body, holding her in place while he pushed his cock deep into her womb. When she shattered with her climax, she bit down on his shoulder to anchor herself as she spun out of control. Her orgasm was stronger than she had ever felt, and she sensed a change in her all the way down to her toes. It was like an invisible string was tied between the two of them that neither could undo.

She lay there silently for several minutes still physically connected to him before she spoke.

"I'm so sorry I bit you, are you okay?" Her worried eyes caught his smile as her fingertips touched the bite wound gently. He laughed softly.

"I'm perfect, Caroline. It's natural for wolves to bite their mates during sex. I loved it when you bit me, and I hope you will do so when we make love in the future. That's how a wolf claims its mate and marks them for the whole world to see. It completes the bond between us." He kissed her on her temple as he shifted off of her, but he didn't let her go. She was surprised when tears started falling from her eyes.

"Thank you, Devin. I've never felt like that. I mean sex has never been…it's just, well…that was beautiful." She heard the emotion in her own voice, and the love in his eyes told her that he did, too. He wiped the tears away and kissed her softly in reassurance.

"You are beautiful, Caroline, and you shouldn't be thanking me. You gave me the best gift I've ever received from anyone. Your love and your mating mark." The moment was so perfect that it almost hurt, and they both lay there silently relishing their spent passion, just enjoying each other's embrace.

"Are you ready to meet the rest of your family yet?" he asked her quietly, hating to ruin the moment.

"Right after I shower…crap…Devin, I don't have any of my clothes! What am I going to wear?" She sat up quickly and turned to look at his smiling face. "What? Do you want to introduce me to your family naked? Is that a wolf thing? I wondered about that when your dad introduced himself naked. I'm not exactly comfortable with all this nudity yet, sorry."

"Hell no, you aren't meeting anyone naked. All your new clothes are still in the truck from our shopping trip yesterday. I brought them in last night before I came up here. They are in the closet, now go take your shower, and get dressed. Mama probably has breakfast ready by now, and if I don't get you down there I'm afraid she will come looking for you. She is anxious to have some girl talk."

Laughing, he rolled out of bed, pulling her along with him, and gave her ass a quick swat as she headed for the bathroom. Within twenty minutes, they were both dressed and ready to go downstairs. He watched her take a big breath, steeling her emotions before she took his hand and squeezed it gently.

"Lead the way, wolf," she said with a flirty grin, and she followed along, keeping her fingers tightly entwined with his. As they entered the large kitchen, Caroline was surprised to see just Sienna and Jim sitting at the dining room table. She had expected a large crowd of people, and was pleased that she could start with just these two.

"Morning," Jim called, noticing them standing in the doorway. He beckoned them over to the table. "Come on over and help yourselves. You know Mama, Dev, she cooked up a storm in honor of your new mate."

Sienna stood and greeted them halfway to the table. Devin kissed his mom on the cheek, and she hugged Caroline before pulling her over to a seat next to hers.

"Yes, I enjoy cooking for my pups. Did you sleep well, Caroline?" Sienna had turned back to the table, and was handing Caroline a platter filled with fried ham, bacon, and sausage. There was also a bowl filled with fruit salad, a platter of pancakes, toast, hash browns, and a large dish of scrambled eggs. Caroline laughed to herself as she could see where the twins had learned to eat.

"I did, thank you. This all looks delicious, and your home is beautiful, Sienna. I can't wait to see more of the den." She filled her plate and settled in comfortably to eat.

"Please dear, call me Mom. I hope you will start to think of Jim and I as family quickly. We already love you as a daughter." Sienna's smile was warm and friendly, and she reached over to pat Caroline's had as she spoke.

"After breakfast I want to call a meeting and have everyone come to the circle so that I can introduce her. I just spoke with Damon, and he should be here any second," Devin said. Surprise filled her, and she stared at Devin, silently wondering why Damon wouldn't have talked to them both through their link.

Because I wanted to surprise you, beautiful, and Dev just went and screwed up the surprise.

Devin rolled his eyes as Damon's words floated into both his and Caroline's heads. Then the front door banged open, and Caroline smelled Damon's scent before she could see him. She felt something inside her reaching for him, and she jumped to her feet, moving toward the doorway before she could stop herself. She fell into Damon's arms just inside the great room, and he kissed her deeply. His hands locked around her waist, and he lifted her just off of her feet. It felt right when she looped her own arms around his neck and wrapped her legs around his waist to deepen the kiss. His tongue swept hers, and his hands moved to cup her ass as he braced her back against the closest wall.

A sudden clearing of a throat interrupted their hot reunion, and they both turned their heads to see Sienna, Jim, and Devin in the kitchen doorway. Sienna's eyes shimmered with tears, and Jim looked like his chest was going to pop it was so swollen up with pride.

"Guess you missed me, huh, beautiful?" Damon asked her, playfully setting her back down on her feet. Caroline blushed hotly, and met his smile with a grin of her own.

"Nope," she said, and everyone but Damon cracked up with laughter. His eyes flashed, and he reached for her.

"Hmmm...well then let's start over and see if you react like before," he said menacingly, but she could see the laughter in his eyes, and knew he had missed her just as much. She grabbed his hand and pulled him toward his waiting parents, laughing the whole way.

"Better take a minute to say hello to your parents first. We can reconvene at a later time." She gave him a flirty smile and blew him a quick kiss to tell him that she wanted him as badly as he wanted her, and he followed her willingly.

Damon greeted both of his parents with hugs and kisses on the cheek, and then sat down next to her at the kitchen table. He scooted his chair as close to her as possible and kept his thigh pressed against hers. She had missed him so deeply while he was separated from her for hours that it had physically begun to hurt. But it looked like he wasn't letting her go far from his side now.

They chatted while they all ate breakfast. Damon and the guys had nothing new to report, and Barton seemed to have covered his trail enough to hide for now. Caroline saw Devin and Damon exchange a look, and she narrowed her eyes at them. They both smiled innocently, but she could tell that there was more to the story than they wanted to share with her. She hoped they would soon realize that she wanted to be included in everything, even the things that they wanted to protect her from.

"Oh yeah, and Tina called for you, beautiful. She said that mine was the only phone number she could track down to get ahold of you. I guess she called the firehouse and got Liam on the phone. Did a number on him, sounds like she is quite a little spitfire," Damon said through a mouthful of food, and swallowing, he laughed, "You should have seen the look on Liam's face when he gave me the message!"

"Oh my god I didn't even think about leaving a different phone number with anyone to get ahold of me. My cell phone was in my purse where I left it the night of the fire. I will have to go to the cell phone store so that they can help me get a new phone. I better go call her and reassure her that you guys didn't kill me, at least not yet anyways." She laughed and took Damon's cell phone from him, pausing for the kiss he brushed across her lips before she headed for the great room.

As she passed by, Devin grabbed her arm, and tugged her face to his for a quick kiss as well. Her breath caught in her throat when she felt his tongue lick across her lips. Pulling back quickly, she laughed at him. His eyes sparked with desire, and held a promise for later. She swatted his hands away, and left the room still laughing. She could hear Devin asking Damon about Liam's conversation with Tina as she drifted out of hearing distance. She made a mental note to get the scoop from Damon later on. She settled onto an oversize ottoman in the middle of the room, and called Tina.

"Caroline! Lord, girl, where have you been? I've been so worried about you. You left the hospital with those two guys, and for all I knew they were serial killers! I mean they would have a great disguise, as hot as they are. No one would suspect them. Then I couldn't reach you, and Carter said he didn't know what happened to you, either. He said some guy came by the hospital asking about you, too. Is everything okay?" Tina's voice was excited and impatient, and Caroline found herself rolling her eyes as she took a deep breath.

"Tina, slow down. I'm fine. I'm great in fact! I'm in love with them, Tina. Devin and Damon are the best things to ever happen to me." She could hear the love in her own voice.

"What? How can you be in love after a couple of days? Caroline, did you hit your head during that fire? Now, don't get me wrong, those two were delicious looking, and I have no doubt they would be a hell of a ride, but in love?" Tina sounded doubtful.

"Trust me, Tina, there is so much more to them than I even realized. I've spent every minute with them for the last few days. I'm at their d...home right now meeting their parents, actually." She almost slipped and called it a den. She wondered what Tina would say to the idea of her good friend falling for a couple of werewolves, and turning into one herself.

"Wow! I'm stunned, Caroline. I've known you for years, and you have never even had an overnight date with a man in that time. You don't jump into anything. So if you are keeping them around for a while...when do I get to meet their hot fireman friends? The one I talked to the other day had a sexy, deep voice. Almost made me ask him out just because of his voice! You've already laid claim to two of the best ones, but surely there is just one more for me?" Tina seemed truly shocked at her best friend's actions, but she laughed along with Caroline as they went on to chat about work. Caroline explained what all had occurred in the last few days, excluding everything wolf related. Caroline was pleased that Tina didn't argue harder for her to step back and think about everything. She was afraid that too many questions would force her to make decisions, and she wasn't ready to make them yet.

They finished their call with a promise that Caroline would talk to the guys and set up a time to get together with her. Now that Caroline had found her happiness, she wanted to see Tina find hers, and she would do anything to help her with it. She thought about her conversation, and realized that she hadn't asked Tina who was at the hospital looking for her, but she shrugged it off, thinking that it was probably just a former patient.

Heading back into the kitchen, she froze just inside the doorway when she realized that the mood had changed completely. Liam, Cash, and Owen all stood around the room with serious looks on their faces. And now instead of the laughing, laid-back family she had left a few minutes ago, a serious and emotional group sat in their place.

"What's wrong?" she asked, her voice breaking just slightly.

"Caroline…" Damon said, but he couldn't go on. He clearly didn't know how to tell her whatever he needed to tell her. He looked at his brother, his eyes pleading with Devin to explain.

"Barton Diego issued a challenge for tomorrow night," Devin said quietly. He stared directly into her brown eyes, just waiting for her reaction. His muscles were tense, and his jaw was clenched.

"What? No! Not yet! Why so fast? I just found you…" Everyone was shocked at the intensity of her reaction. She was yelling at him! Devin was stunned because she always seemed so calm and together, but now her emotions danced in her eyes, plain for all to see.

Devin watched her as she struggled with her own reaction. Her eyes had turned to liquid chocolate and were filled with fear, and her body trembled. His gut twisted because he knew she was scared, and he couldn't reassure her. She was just going to have to understand. He was a wolf, and an Alpha wolf at that. He had to protect his pack, and he had to prove his worthiness to lead them. He would face Barton, no matter what the result.

"It's not a choice, Caroline. I will face Barton tomorrow night, and I will kill him. Then we will plan our wedding." He said it with more control than he even knew he was capable of. The fear and sadness in her eyes, and the silent tears falling down her cheeks were almost his undoing.

"Caroline, there is more to this challenge than you understand…" Damon started to say, but he paused when his brother shook his head at him.

"Then make me understand. What has changed that made this guy want to have the challenge so fast?" She kept her confused eyes on Damon, refusing to let him off the hook.

"He wants you, beautiful," Damon said, his heart breaking with every word as she went completely pale. "He issued the challenge to Devin for you. It's not a challenge just for the pack leader. He made it clear that he has scented you and desires you for his mate."

"What? I thought once mated that a wolf couldn't mate someone else." she said in a whisper. When no one spoke immediately, she shifted onto one hip and crossed her arms, her gaze moving from one man to the next until she had looked at all five of the guys in front of her. Sienna moved up beside her and put a hand on her shoulder in comfort.

Liam was the one that answered her question, and she watched him as he shifted uncomfortably under her gaze. "It's not that they can't mate someone else, but usually they don't have the desire to. A claiming bite mark on a wolf from their mate is like a warning light to other wolves. Wolves mate for life, and once claimed, other wolves don't usually challenge the bond, but Barton isn't a normal wolf. He is crazy in his hatred for Devin, and he may be stupid enough to try to get to you." The silence was oppressive as she realized that Barton Diego was intending on killing Devin to get to her, and that he wasn't going to take no for an answer if he reached her. A small shiver of terror went through her spine. A dark thought slipped into her mind.

What if Barton just wanted her? What if she offered herself to him to protect Devin? She would do anything to protect her men, even if it meant sacrificing herself.

"The hell you will." Damon and Devin both stood and glowered at her. She knew they had heard her thoughts. Anger glowed in their faces, but she tipped her chin defiantly at them. Everyone else watched in confusion.

"I will do whatever necessary to protect you," she said angrily.

"You will not put your life at risk. This is not negotiable, Caroline. As our mate, you are as important to the pack as we are, and you risk more than you know if you attempt anything so stupid." Devin's voice was an angry growl, and his normally light-green eyes were darkened with rage.

"Stupid? You think loving you is stupid? Well hell, maybe it is! Maybe the stupidest thing I've done in my life is fall in love with you and your brother." Her tears still fell from her cheeks, and she could feel the intense pain of her heartbreak. She just wanted to protect them like they wanted to protect her.

"Stop it. Both of you," Damon yelled at them. Reaching out, he held Caroline's hands in his own loose grip and waited for her to meet his eyes. "Caroline, you are the best thing that ever happened to the two of us. We both love you so much that we want to protect you from everything, but we can't do that if you won't protect yourself. I need to explain something to you. Once mated a wolf is stronger in every way because it shares its soul with its mate. It has both pieces of its heart, and that increases its strength. If you were to pull away from Devin now, right before the challenge, it would weaken him. He won't admit it, but he needs you. He needs you to be strong for him. Not fight him on this."

Everyone held their breath. Caroline glanced around the room, seeing the truth on the sad faces around her. Finally turning back to her men, she sighed heavily, and closed her eyes. Why was this happening to them? She had spent so much of her life sad and alone, and now that she finally had someone to live for, she might have to give them up, too. She could feel the weight of her depression in her chest, and she fought to control the darkness so that it wouldn't envelope her heart again. She would go along with this until she could come up with a better plan, because she couldn't bring herself to chance hurting her men. If what Damon said was true, then she needed to put on a brave face for now.

"Fine. Sienna, I believe someone was going to introduce me to the pack, and after I go clean up a bit I want to meet them." Meeting Devin's icy green eyes, she glared at him as she brushed away the last of her tears. "Understand this. I will do everything in my power to stop this. I just found you two, and I'm not ready to give you up." She spun on her heel and stomped off to the bathroom.

Damon stood open mouthed watching Caroline exit the room. As much as he hated to admit it, her desire to protect Devin was a blatant reaction of love. After a moment of silence while everyone absorbed her reaction to the news, Devin took a deep breath of his own before issuing orders.

"Betas, please send the word that we will meet at the circle in one hour. Everyone should be there, no exceptions. I plan to continue my day just like I would have before this challenge, and introduce the pack to my future wife." He walked away from all of them in the opposite direction of Caroline, leaving everyone shocked in his wake. It took all Damon's strength not to go to Caroline and console her, but he needed some time to think himself, too.

"I told you she was perfect for us. It takes a lot of courage, and a lot of pride to be the Alpha's mate." Damon's voice swelled with his pride, and he smiled sadly to his parents and cousins.

"We will make sure she is protected, Damon. We will set up around-the-clock watches for the whole den." Owen was already formulating a plan to reinforce their security.

"I know that, guys. I trust you to protect her as you would any of our family. I also know that we can't protect her from herself. I just hope she doesn't let her pride get her into trouble. Barton is a sick fuck, and he will do everything he can to make this an unfair fight." He felt slightly lost as he looked toward the doorway that Caroline had just stomped through.

Liam, Cash, and Owen exchanged a look, and then, shaking their heads, they left the cabin to pass the word throughout the pack about the meeting.

Caroline stood in front of the bathroom mirror with a cold, wet washcloth on her forehead trying hard to control her emotions and mentally prepare herself for meeting the pack. She was scared, and angry. She wanted to spend more time with her men before this challenge happened. What if something happened to Devin? What would that mean for her, his mate? She could already feel the wolf inside of her, getting stronger, and becoming a part of her like her arms were. They had told her that if a wolf died, his mate would usually soon follow, but what did that mean for a wolf with a mate who already had another mate? Would both she and Damon die if Devin did? Would she survive and be forced to endure a life mated with the man that killed her true love? It was all too much to swallow, and she wanted to curl up in a ball and cry herself to sleep.

A knock at the bathroom door abruptly killed her pity party, and she wiped her face free of tears before opening the door to see who was there. To her surprise it was Jim, the twins' father, and former Alpha of the pack.

"You okay, Caroline?" He smiled a warm smile at her, and she could see the sadness in his eyes.

"Yes, I will be fine. Thank you, Jim. I just need a few minutes to pull it together before I get thrown to the wolves." He laughed at her joke and then pulled her to his chest to hug her. She melted into the embrace, and wondered at how different it was than when her men held her. This was reminiscent of when her father would hold her as a child. A wave of despair hit her as she grieved for all the hugs she had missed out on.

"I'm so glad to have you here, Caroline. I can see how much my sons mean to you, and I know how much you mean to them. You need to trust in Devin when he says that he has this challenge under control. If I believed he wouldn't win, then I would volunteer to fight in his place, but he is a stronger wolf than I have ever been or could have hoped to be. I once thought there was no chance he would find a woman who could break through his walls and reach his heart, but he found you. Please try to be patient with him, because this has been a change for all three of you." His words comforted her heart, and she hugged him back, thinking about how much he smelled like her men. He was the same build and height, but his hair was salt-and-pepper gray, and he was not as muscular anymore. She decided she was glad to call him family, and she reached up on her toes to kiss his cheek.

"Thank you, for sharing that. I am scared, but I will be okay. I've been through worse heartbreak in my life and survived. Now please introduce me to my new family." He looped his arm through hers, and they headed out of the cabin.

He pointed out various things along the way to the circle. There were many different cabins scattered throughout the woods, each at the end of a gravel drive that split off the main road. None of the cabins were as large as the one the Alpha wolves stayed in, but they were all lovely and fit into the scenery perfectly. Walking along the main road, she could see dozens of wolves and people moving along the same road in the same direction. As they rounded a large bend in the road, they came upon a clearing that was a perfect circle shape. All around the circle there were boulders and large stones that wolves and people alike sat upon. In the center was a platform with a set of wooden stairs leading up to it. She could see Devin, Damon, Cash, and Ryley all standing next to it, and she followed her instincts and went to them. The people around her parted as if understanding her place in the hierarchy already.

As she reached them, both men reached out to her together. They held her between them, and took the time to look into her eyes, and then each kissed her softly.

"I love you so much," Devin whispered against her temple while he held her tightly against his chest. Damon nuzzled her neck, and she could feel all the anger of their argument dissolve. Emotion overwhelmed her, and she just stood there immersed in their love for a few moments.

"I know, wolf. I know," she whispered back, and, smiling softly at him, she let him lead her up the stairs.

At the top of the platform with Damon at her back and Devin at her side, she looked around. The trees that enclosed the circle were tall, and their thick trunks told her they were old. There were easily seventy-five werewolves in various forms in the clearing, and more filed in as they prepared to start. Her nerves balled up in her gut, and her palms were sweating because she hated being in front of a crowd. The scents were overwhelming to her new wolf senses, but she was startled to realize that she could now specifically pick out certain ones. She could smell her men. They were beside her so that wasn't surprising, but she could also pick out Rafe who stood in the back, and smiled encouragingly when she met his gaze. Then she picked up on Liam to her right who saluted her when he caught her attention, and he winked, smiling his charming smile at her. She saw him lean over and whisper to a beautiful raven-haired woman who stood next to him, and she briefly wondered who the woman was. She didn't think any of the men from the firehouse were mated yet, but she hadn't ever asked. The reassuring smiles of Jim and Sienna were next in her line of sight, and she found herself relaxing in spite of being in front of so many eyes.

Devin raised his hand, and the crowd went silent. Everyone waited quietly to hear what he had to say, even the handful of children. He took a breath and spoke, his voice a rumbling echo throughout the trees.

"Family, I have collected you here for two reasons, one bad, and one wonderful. The first is to let you know that I have received word of an Alpha challenge for tomorrow night." The crowd growled its frustration and anger at this first announcement, and Caroline took a small step backward. Damon placed his hands at her waist, pulling her back snugly against his chest. His warmth reassured her that she wasn't facing this alone. Her men were behind her in every way. She wanted to reach for Devin and reassure him that he wasn't alone, but she didn't know if it was appropriate in front of his family.

She jumped a bit, startled out of her thoughts when Devin raised his hand to calm the group and continued, "The challenger is Barton Diego. I have no fear of this challenge, and my intention is to deal with it quickly and thoroughly."

There was some laughter as many recognized the implied threat of his words. He smiled a small smile, and then reached for her hand. Reassured and calmed by his gentle touch, she smiled up at him. He brought her fingers to his lips and then looked back to the crowd. "The second reason is to introduce you to Caroline Trainor—soon to be Gray. She is my mate as well as Damon's mate, and the newest member of the Gray Pack."

Again the crowd came alive, but this time instead of growling, she heard cheering! She heard whistles and laughter, and too many congratulations and welcomes to acknowledge them all. She felt tears behind her eyelids as she was openly welcomed into this new family. They all seemed to be genuinely happy to have her. She couldn't imagine a better way to start her new life. She forced herself not to think about the fact that she hadn't actually agreed to be a permanent member of the Gray Pack yet, and instead she let the warmth of the group melt her insides.

"Now, I plan to bring her around to meet everyone individually… eventually, but for now I just ask that you give us some time together as a newly mated family. Please embrace her as one of our own, and I know you will love her as much as Damon and I do." Caroline blushed at his words as she heard catcalls, and one significantly loud whistle that she knew came from Liam.

The crowd suddenly went eerily quiet as a beautiful woman stepped up to the stairs, and bent one knee in submission, awaiting permission to approach them on the platform. The twins exchanged a look over Caroline's head, and then Devin nodded to the woman, allowing her to move up to stand next to them. She took Caroline's hands in hers, and bent at the waist to lean down and kiss them.

"I want to welcome you, Caroline, as Devin and Damon's mate, to your new family," she said in a soft, melodious voice as she looked straight into Caroline's eyes. She admired the lovely woman, and wondered who she could be. She looked about the same age as herself, but her blue eyes appeared to be much older. They held a wisdom in them that she had never seen up close. Her hair was almost white blonde, as were her eyebrows and eyelashes. Her eyes were blue, but so light in color that they were almost white. Her cheeks had a soft tinge of pink to them that proved to Caroline that there was blood in her veins. She was petite like Caroline, but she seemed more fragile some-how. Her hands were small and soft, and her smell was delicate and lovely. Caroline felt immediately at ease as she looked into this woman who smiled warmly at her.

Who? Caroline couldn't resist asking her men silently.

Her name is Delaky. In the human world she would be called a shaman. She has magic in her, and knows the wisdom of our ancestors as well. Her blessing guarantees your acceptance into the pack. Don't be afraid, she will not hurt you. Damon's words strummed a chord in Caroline, clearly this woman was very important in the pack. Something inside of her made her very eager to talk with Delaky and get to know her.

Later, my dear. Come to me later, and we will visit. Your mates will know where to find me.

Delaky laughed softly when Caroline's mouth dropped open at hearing a new voice in her head. She had no idea that it was possible for anyone but Devin and Damon to converse with her in such a way. It was slightly intimidating. As Delaky released Caroline's hands, she turned back to the crowd, and in a rippling fashion they all knelt and bowed their heads. It took Caroline a moment to realize that they were paying obeisance to her as their leader's new mate, as well as acknowledging their beloved shaman's acceptance of her. She was in awe of the action, and for a moment her throat tightened with emotion. Looking at Delaky, she swallowed hard. Delaky gestured to the crowd, indicating that it was Caroline's turn to speak. Shakily she stepped forward, and her eyes roamed over the now kneeling crowd.

"Thank you. I hope that I can make you all as proud of me, as I am of you already," she said to the assembly, and was pleased when they all cheered again. Devin's smile told her that she had said the right thing, and she was assured of it again when Damon bent to kiss the top of her head. The crowd started to scatter as her men helped her down the stairs. Waiting at the bottom were all of the guys from the firehouse, Sienna, and Jim. They took turns hugging her, and they all shared a laugh when Liam hugged her just a few extra moments before letting her go with a soft tap on her ass. Both Devin and Damon growled their threat, and then laughed as well when they caught on to the joke. The dark-haired woman that had stood with Liam was introduced as his sister, Whitney, and Caroline took an immediate liking to the confident woman.

I had forgotten what family felt like. I missed it. She sent her thought to her men, and they both looked at her curiously. They didn't know much about her past, and they were instantly aware of that lack of knowledge. There was more to her that they needed to know, and soon.

CHAPTER TWELVE

After spending the rest of the day meeting the various werewolves and their families, Caroline's head was spinning again. She hoped she would be able to remember everyone's names soon. There were so many of them. Everyone she met had welcomed her with smiles and even hugs. Thinking back over her life, she remembered the affection of her parents with each other, and felt their loss poignantly. They had always held hands and cuddled with each other. She couldn't remember a day passing that they didn't say I love you to each other, and to her. She understood it more now, because with Devin and Damon it just seemed natural to walk along holding their hands or sneaking a kiss and a cuddle every chance they got. She relished the easy way they would reach out with an arm and pull her closer to their sides if she moved too far away. She felt the need to be close and touch them as well, and they seemed to glow with approval when she would initiate a touch. She could feel Damon's hand on the small of her back, and Devin's fingers looped through the belt loop on the back of her jeans in a possessive way. The spark of heat those small touches created in her belly was close to being a bonfire by afternoon, and she started to feel agitated at having to continue the meet and greet with the pack.

She turned her attention to Damon and was overwhelmingly pleased to see the passion reflected there. She tried to convey her needs to him without speaking or thinking them. Hoping he could read it in her eyes and her touch. She preened when he got the message loud and clear.

"Okay, let's go. It's time for you to stop thinking for a while. I think I know just how to help you relax." As he said it her clit throbbed with desire, and her lips parted unintentionally. The gleam in his eyes told her that he wanted her as much as she wanted him, and by God they were finally going to do something about it. He pressed tightly against her back and spoke just loud enough for both Devin and her to hear him.

"I would love to stop thinking for a bit. How are you planning on turning me on…I mean off?" She grinned at her intentional slip of the tongue, and the guys laughed. She was so easy to read, and they loved that she was so blunt about her desires.

"For starters, I want to get you away from everyone else and into a quiet place. Then I plan to use my hands, my tongue, and my cock to make you scream my name until I'm all your mind can handle." His voice had dropped an octave and was husky with heat now as his hands came around her waist and cupped her mound. He pressed his middle fingers against the denim of her jeans and could feel her heat. She moaned, and instantly arched her butt back against his now rock-hard cock. His callused fingertips moved to run over the slim line of bare skin at the bottom edge of her tank top, and she shivered with anticipation. She almost looked down to check and see if there were scorch marks left on her skin.

"What are we waiting for?" she asked impatiently. They both laughed again, and she frowned at them.

"Unfortunately, I have to do some things right now, sugar, so I will leave you in Damon's capable hands. Don't have so much fun that you don't rest. I want you to be able to revisit this discussion when I'm available later. Damon, don't forget we promised to take her to Delaky's later tonight," he said, and he kissed her deeply before turning her to face Damon and then smacked her ass just hard enough to draw a whimper from her. She couldn't hide the disappointment from her eyes as she watched him walk away toward yet another group of pack members. She had hoped for an afternoon of delight with her men. She turned to Damon to see what his reaction would be.

"Well, now what?" she asked and planted her hands on her rounded hips, cocking them to one side in irritation.

"I get you all to myself, beautiful, and I can't wait to play with you until you beg for me to let you come." His voice was low so that no one but her could have heard him, and she felt her cheeks flush with the heat. She reached out with one hand to take his, and he pulled her along behind him.

To her surprise, Damon led her past the main cabin along a footpath for a few minutes, going deeper into the forest. This part of the forest was cooler, and darker, and it smelled so fresh. The path they were on became rocky and a bit more overgrown, and she looked up to see Damon in front of her pulling the branches of a bush out of the way for her.

As she moved through another opening he made for her, she gasped. The clearing in front of them was painfully beautiful. There was a small creek that meandered through this hideaway in the woods, and it widened into a decent-sized pool of water in a crescent shape. The pool looked to be deep enough to sink into, and there was a large flat rock perched at the edge. In her mind she could already feel the cold stone on the back of her thighs and knew what the cool water would feel like if she sank her feet in. There were tall trees surrounding the spot on all four sides, and just the whisper of sunlight fell on a thick patch of clovers along the bank of the creek. It was romantic, secluded, and she could feel the magic of the space. Her eyes met Damon's, and she felt her heart swelling with the love she saw reflected in his eyes.

"Do you like it?" he whispered as he moved up against her, and tipped her head back so that she could look up into his eyes.

"I love it! This place is amazing! Thank you so much for sharing it with me!" she whispered back. Even though she knew that they were completely alone and no one would hear her words, it just seemed like this space was a space for quiet reflection and intimate passions.

Damon silently walked her over to the large stone and began removing their clothes. He spread his shirt out on top of the rock, moving her gently until she lay on her back. She stretched out, enjoying the fire in his eyes as he devoured the sight of her naked body in the shadows of the trees. She felt feminine and sexy under his hot gaze. Her nipples pebbled and ached with need. She ran her finger-nails gently over the peaks, hearing her own husky moan, and he quickly spread himself over her prone form, replacing her hands with his own on her breasts. His face was taut with need, and he kissed her gently before his hands started to explore her body. His stiff erection brushed against the soft skin of her inner thigh, and they both groaned.

"Damon, oh God..." she whimpered at him, and he lifted his head. Her hands reached out to hold him, and she tangled her fingers in the soft hair at the nape of his neck. Her hands drifted over his broad shoulders, memorizing every curve and taut muscle. She loved touching him and feeling the passionate ripples of his muscles as he moved. Sliding her arms around him to explore the bunched muscles of his shoulders and lower back, she wanted him so much she could barely catch her breath.

"Shhhh...let me love you, Caroline. I want to love you." His voice rumbled through, melting her to the bone.

His open-mouthed kiss was loving and intoxicating. Drawing on her tongue hard, and then reversing the move with his own tongue, he imitated the thrusting that she desperately craved. She let her head fall back as his lips lavished kisses down the column of her throat. His fingers danced over every secret her body held until she arched up against him. He pressed his palm against her mound and slid his finger through her creamy slit, using her own wetness to slip his finger farther between the soft swells of her ass to her rosebud. She squealed as he let the tip of his finger press into the tight ring of muscles before he moved back to her aching clit. She pressed her hard pink nipple against his cheek and he sucked it into his mouth using his lips to pull her toward him. When he let go, it fell from his mouth with a loud popping sound. The other nipple was next, but this one he nipped with his teeth, eliciting a sharp gasp from her. His fingers never stopped fluttering softly at her folds, but he wasn't penetrating her yet, and she was starting to burn for an orgasm.

She rocked her hips up against his muscular stomach, and felt the tip of his hard cock brush her ass cheeks. She shivered with need as she threaded her fingers deeper into his hair and held him tight against her breast. He slid one finger deep into her cleft and used his thumb to softly tease her ass. She moaned, and her breathing became rough pants as he teased her to the brink. Just as she felt the edge of her orgasm start, he pulled his hand away from her and sat up so that he could look at her face. He was grinning devilishly as she glared back at him.

"What are you doing?" She panted, her frustration clearly evident in her voice.

"Not yet, beautiful. I don't want you just moaning. I want you screaming my name when you come." He proceeded to pull her dainty foot up to his mouth and plant a kiss on the arch. She hadn't realized how sensitive her feet were, and couldn't hold back her groans as his soft kisses moved up her ankle and calf. He spent several moments at the back of her knee when it caused her to make soft mewling sounds. Just when she thought she was going to die with need, he moved his mouth right where she wanted it. His tongue slid through her hot cream, and stroked her swollen clit. She cried out, and gasped for breath as she locked her ankles behind his head and grabbed her breasts, pinching her own nipples tightly. Her cries weren't words, but the sound sent the message.

"That's it, Caroline, tell me what you want. I love tasting your pussy." He purred the words against her softness, and she could feel his hot breath caressing her vibrating pearl. His fingers skimmed over her rosebud, and then gently caressed the globes of her ass as his tongue tickled her clit. She writhed hard against him, trying to reach for her peak, but every time she would get close, he would pull back a little.

"Please, Damon, I need you. Stop teasing me, and fuck me! Please!" She was whimpering with desire now as she tried to guide him back up her body by tugging at his hair, and shoulders.

"Your wish is my command, beautiful," he said, lifting himself above her to thrust his thickness balls deep into her. She could feel him against her womb, and she screamed out loud. His eyes darkened to almost black at her obvious pleasure, and he began to thrust into her hard. His hands gripped her hips tightly, and her hands wrapped around his wrists to hold him close. Her soft thighs locked at his waist, and her breasts bounced with every thrust he made. He tilted his hips so that the head of his dick rubbed right against her G-spot, stroking her until she squealed and whimpered.

"That's it. Come on, beautiful. Come for me. Now!" His gasping words were barely clear in her brain as he pushed into her. Her orgasm burst in her brain like fireworks, and her vision dimmed. She felt an electric shock roll through her as his seed splashed deep inside her body, and she bit down on his shoulder as she shattered into pieces. The internal fire consumed her at the taste of his blood on her tongue, and she was lost. She drifted into darkness with a feminine, satisfied smile on her face.

Damon lifted his head a few moments later when he realized Caroline's breathing had evened out, and he almost laughed out loud at his sleeping mate. She had finally claimed him, and his heart soared. The mating bond between the three of them was complete. Devin had shown him the mark that he now carried from their lovemaking this morning, and Damon had been inexplicably jealous, but now he was elated. As he watched her sleep, he wondered if she really understood what the bite meant when she did it, and he finally decided that he didn't really care. She loved them, and they loved her, and she wasn't going anywhere.

He pulled away from her and spread her shirt over her as a blanket. Even though this clearing was secluded and few people knew it was here, he didn't think she would be too happy if someone found her naked and spread out on a rock. Then he dropped into the pool as quietly as he could. He washed the sweat and semen from his body and then just drifted in the pool on his back, enjoying the sounds of the woods.

As he floated in the water, his mind wasn't far from his beautiful mate. She had brought him so much happiness and peace in his life. He wished he knew how to express that to her. When he held her in his arms that first time in the middle of a blazing fire and a collapsing building, he had felt her in his soul. Her scent reached deep inside of him and gripped him tightly, refusing to let go.

All his life he had been second to Devin, but only because of a five minute gap in their births. He had wondered many times at the irony of those five minutes. How would his life have been different if it had been him and not Devin first? Not that it would have changed who he was mated to, but until today he had doubted whether or not she shared the same strong feelings for him that she had for Devin. With that one moment and that one bite, she had bared her soul to him, and he knew that he could never let her go.

He thought about the tournament tomorrow night, and he knew that if Devin were killed, it would mean that Damon would have to challenge Barton Diego himself. He couldn't let that wolf get ahold of Caroline, or the Gray Pack, even if it meant risking his life after watching his brother sacrifice his. How would Caroline feel if he were forced to make that choice? There was no doubt in his mind that she would die shortly of a broken heart if they were not successful in this challenge. She was too closely bonded to them now, and she didn't even really understand it. He had to believe that

Devin would win and that Barton would be gone from their lives forever.

Surely, Delaky could help them explain more to her, and help her to understand that she had already made her final decision to bond with them, even if it was subconscious. He couldn't wait to marry Caroline, and be able to call her wife. He could picture her now coming down the aisle in a beautiful white dress. It amazed him how quickly everything in his life had changed. He was mated now, and so thoroughly besotted with his mate that he didn't stop thinking about her during the day. The moment she had spoken to the pack was the proudest he had ever been, and he could only hope that she would be as proud to call him husband.

He climbed out of the water when he could smell that sunset was approaching and the shadows in the forest were lengthening, moving to wake Caroline. She stretched and arched her back as she woke, and he enjoyed the private smile she gave him when she finally met his eyes. He kissed her softly, and then started to put his clothing back on. As he stood in front of her pulling his jeans on, she stared at the claiming bite mark that branded his shoulder.

"Damon? Did I bite you?" she asked tentatively, her eyes were wide with trepidation, and he smiled at her.

"Yep, and you couldn't have made me happier, beautiful." He bent and kissed her forehead.

"Oh." She paused and looked away. He usually loved watching her emotions flitting across her face, but this time he realized that silent tears were falling from her cheeks. He quickly dropped to his knees next to her, lifting her face until she had to look into his eyes.

"What is it, Caroline? What's wrong? You didn't hurt me, baby, you did just what you should do." He couldn't keep his heart from breaking as he saw the sadness in her eyes. "Why are you so sad, beautiful?"

What is wrong with our mate?

Damon ignored Devin's question as he waited for her response. He couldn't answer because he didn't know, but just like Devin he could feel her withdrawal.

"Damon, I love you. I want to be what you and Devin need, but I just don't think that I can." She pulled her knees up and wrapped her arms around them, sobbing as she dropped her head to rest on them.

"Caroline, you are what we need. Why are you so scared to accept that?" He stroked her hair softly, unsure of what his next step should be. He wanted to wrap her in his arms, but her body language told him that she would pull away.

"I'm a regular person, Damon. I'm a nurse at the hospital in town. I work twelve-hour shifts, and then I go home and put on comfy pajamas and fix a microwave dinner before I settle onto the couch and watch television. I babysit for my next-door neighbor because I'm lonely, and I volunteer occasionally at the local library for story time because I love children." She jumped up from the rock, quickly pulling her clothes on, and started to pace as she ranted. She was finally letting out all her fears, and he needed to hear them. "In my normal life I don't go out dancing, and I don't like to be in front of crowds. I'm not royal, and I'm not sure I can be. I don't want any of us to get hurt, but I can't walk away from everything I know and spend every day waiting for you or Devin to pop into the house for a quick fuck before heading back to the firehouse."

A loud growl sounded at her last statement, and she spun around to see Devin coming into the clearing looking pissed off. He was so large, and when he was angry, he looked dangerous and deadly. She shrank back for a moment before remembering why she had been upset. She tilted her chin up at him, and her eyes squinted in anger. She wasn't going to be bullied or seduced into submission this time.

"What the hell are you talking about? Why would you think that we wanted to use you for a quick fuck? Haven't we made it clear that we want to keep you forever? We don't want a love slave, damn it, Caroline, we want a wife." His face and eyes had darkened with anger, but he held his body with a tight control. He hadn't moved more than a foot or two into the clearing, but his anger sent her heart racing.

"Who the hell is going to marry me, Devin? You or Damon? Exactly how am I going to list that on my emergency contact papers at the hospital where I work? Call one of my *two* husbands if I die? We wouldn't ever be able to live our lives out in the open again. I would always be afraid that people would be judging us." Her voice was full of sorrow. Damon stood and moved toward her with his hands out.

"Caroline? Why do you care what other people think? It is perfectly natural for wolves to take multiple mates." He spoke softly like she was a frightened animal and might attack at any second. She pushed his hands away from her and moved closer to Devin just trying to put distance between her and Damon.

"I'm not a fucking wolf, Damon! I'm a human! I'm a woman! I'm a nurse! *And I'm scared!*" She collapsed to her knees and sobbed into her hands as the two men stared at her, stunned.

Devin's anger seemed to melt, and he quickly moved to her. He scooped her up into his arms, sitting down on the rock next to the pool and cuddling her tightly against his chest as she fell apart emotionally. When her sobbing had slowed to quiet hiccups, he loosened his grip and waited for her to lift her eyes up to his.

"Why are you pushing us away, Caroline?" he asked her, refusing to let her look away until she sighed and started to speak.

"I can't stand to lose either one of you. If I let this happen, and let you into my heart and into my life, then I will break into pieces when I lose you. Loving someone hurts so much, and I can't do it." She spoke with strength in her voice, trying to assure the men that she was serious, and they both gaped at her.

"Caroline, you can't be serious? You would walk away from love because you are afraid it might hurt?" Damon's voice was barely a whisper, and it tore at her resilience. She refused to respond, and after a few moments she pulled out of Devin's embrace and turned to him.

"I can't hurt anymore. I won't survive it." Her words were quiet, but they tore into the men who just stared at her shell-shocked. The twins shared a look of pain as they watched her finish dressing and putting on her shoes. She stood and took a deep breath. "Come on. We promised Delaky we would be meet her tonight. I would like a chance to speak with her."

"And then what happens, Caroline?" Devin said, refusing to let her move away from him with a hand on her hip.

"I don't know yet, Devin. I just don't know." Her voice broke with emotion, but she wiped the last of her tears away and lifted her head to stare blankly at him. Whatever he saw or didn't see in her eyes made him shake his head and he took her hand. Damon moved toward her and took her other hand. She felt their hesitation, and she knew that they both wanted to say more, but she wasn't sure she could listen right now. Her brain was telling her to go back to the cabin and call Tina. She should just get away from here, and away from these men who had a hold over her. Her heart broke at the thought of living without them. Forcefully pulling herself free from their grips, she started walking back toward the path, and the two men followed silently.

After a little ways Devin moved in front of her, leaving Damon walking behind her. They were an implied barrier of protection to anyone looking as they led her down a side path that she hadn't noticed before. After about five minutes the path opened up to another clearing. This one held a very small cabin that had a rocking chair on the front porch, and a laundry line tied between the eaves of the house and a nearby tree. There were wildflowers everywhere, and they bordered the house like a colorful fence. It was pretty, and she bent to pluck a daisy from next to the step as they walked up to the front door. It opened before Devin could knock, and Delaky stood there with a serious look on her face.

"Please come in, children. I can see we have much to discuss, and very little time for decisions." She walked into the house without waiting to see if they followed. Devin held his hand out to Caroline, but instead of taking it she moved past him into the dimly lit room. Delaky now sat on a small wicker bench next to a large stone fireplace. She patted the seat next to her, indicating that Caroline should sit with her. The two men pulled chairs over closer to them from the small kitchen table, and straddling them, they turned to the women.

"Thank you, Delaky, for meeting with us. Thank you also for your blessing upon our mating at Caroline's introduction today." Devin spoke with a deep tone of reverence for the small woman in front of him. Delaky didn't respond immediately. Instead she looked long and hard at each of them before frowning deeply and giving a rough grunt.

"I can see the bond is strong within the three of you, but there are shadows in your light. Why are you fighting your own destiny, my child?" She looked deeply into Caroline's eyes, and when she didn't receive an answer, Delaky spoke again. "Stubborn pride. It is foolishness. You feel pain for the past, and still hold anger in your heart. The fears you have are unfounded. You must let yourself speak the truth to your mates. Let them share your burden."

Caroline's stomach dropped to her feet, and she started to tremble as tears formed in her eyes. "I have told them the truth."

"You have only given them a piece of your truth, and without the whole it means nothing. Give them your pain, and you will be better for it." Delaky's voice was a soothing caress over Caroline's soul, and she looked over at the brothers. They sat spellbound, listening to the shaman speak. When they looked back at Caroline, she could see the confusion, the questions, the fear, and the love in their eyes. She couldn't make her mouth work to tell them. She hadn't shared her past with many people because her grief for her parents was so overwhelming. She couldn't stand it if they saw her grief and depression as a weakness, and turned her away.

Delaky watched her closely, and then said, "Your men have explained to you the bond a wolf has with its mate, am I correct?"

Caroline nodded, and she pressed on, "You have claimed them. I can see their marks. You love them?" It was a question but she didn't wait for a verbal answer. "Eons ago the first wolf claimed his mate from the human world. He met her in a forest where she was picking berries, and upon catching her scent his wolf fought him to claim her. They loved passionately, and with their whole existence, but they were not accepted by her people. She was a princess in her world, but they were banished when her people found out what he was. They faced dangers, and yet they fought because they were two halves of a whole. They each carried a piece of each other in their souls, and would not have survived without the other. They had children, and their children had children, and so the first pack was born. It is said that they died in each other's arms in their old age, because neither could give the other up to the next life to exist alone. It is that bond that you now have with your mates. If you choose to continue to withhold a piece of yourself, you will never have room for the pieces of soul they want to give to you."

Delaky turned abruptly to the men. "And how honest have you been with your mate? Have you taught her the ways of the wolf? Have you opened her eyes to our world or have you just shared pieces of your world and your passion with her? How can she build a future on questions? She does not know her place in our pack, and so she balks at the responsibility heaped upon her back. You are at fault for her unease."

"It's happened so fast…" Damon started, but Delaky jumped to her feet and brushed his statement away.

"Bah! You are scared children, and none of you are willing to risk the pain for the pleasure. Love is a gift, but it comes with a responsibility. A child is not ready, and so I find you. Caroline, you are of a giving nature. You want a family. I see two paths for you, and you are at the crossroads where you must choose the one which is right for you. I see births and deaths in your future, no matter the direction you choose. But…should you choose the correct path and face the challenges that come with it, the wolf will guide you. Life is what you choose it to be, but you must choose soon."

Caroline felt the hot tears running down her cheeks, as she turned to the fireplace and stared into the dancing flames. There was so much she needed them to know, so that they could understand where she was coming from. Delaky could see into her soul, or she wouldn't have pushed her so hard. She let all her emotions come to the surface, and she started to speak.

"I'm sorry, Devin and Damon. I don't mean to keep things from you, and you both know that I love you with all my heart. But I have baggage. More baggage than I have ever even admitted to myself. My parents were killed in the World Trade Center. They were the most loving people I have ever known, but they were very absorbed in each other. I was the only child of two only children. They only had one child because my dad couldn't stand to see my mom go through labor and delivery again. He loved her so deeply, but so selfishly. Believe me when I say that I know that I was loved, and they told me so daily. But they were distant from me at the same time. They didn't hug me or cuddle me, and when I got ready for my senior prom my mom didn't even help me dress. She and Dad were planning a date night and couldn't be bothered to even take pictures of my date and I." She began to pace as she spoke trying to get all the words out before she fell apart.

Out of the corner of her eye she could see Delaky give a slight nod to her to continue, "Even without the affection that I needed from them, they were still my whole world. I don't have any other family, and when they died I lost my love for life. I lost my grasp on reality. I fell into such a deep depression that it took me almost five years to get out of it. I was suicidal at times, I was angry and hurt, and I felt so much pain. I went back to school for my degree and became a nurse because I had nightmares about being at ground zero with my parents lying on the ground dying. In my dreams I couldn't help them because I didn't know how. I need to help people, and I have found that being a nurse fills a void I have carried since they died. You need a mate that can give you everything she is, and become your support. How can I do that for you without giving up what I need? I'm terrified that I would have to live through that grief again if you were killed in the challenge tomorrow, Devin. I don't think I could survive it again."

She met Damon's eyes first, but couldn't hold his gaze when she saw the sheen of tears there. Devin's eyes held sympathy, and regret, but not pity like she anticipated. She tipped her chin at him daring him to challenge her feelings.

"Caroline, you have been exposed to an unbearable tragedy in your life, but we want to help you get past the grieving, and learn to live again. We both love you with every ounce of our being, and we are committed to doing anything to protect you and show you that we will take care of you." Devin's words were laced with pain and frustration.

"Would you pull out of the challenge, Devin? Would you stop this madness if I asked you to? If I told you that I would open myself up to loving you, and give up my old life completely, would you sacrifice your pride for me?" She didn't beg, and her voice didn't even carry a hint of the pleading need she felt inside, because she already knew the answer.

"No. I can't walk away from this challenge, Caroline. My pack is on the line. My family is on the line. Damn it, Caroline, our whole existence is on the line. We love you, but if you don't love us enough to accept us as we are…then I agree with you that we must stop lying to ourselves about how easy this will all be. We can't go on pretending and wishing it would change." His eyes drifted over Damon's bite mark that she had left behind, and Damon's pissed-off expression.

"I wish it were different. I want a family of my own. I want to have children and my career, too. If I were to stay I would be giving up a piece of me, and I'm afraid I will resent you both for it. I have responsibilities in my real life that I must go back to. I have to work because I have to pay the bills. I need to go back to reality and stop living in this fantasy." She spoke to them as much as to herself, and then she stood and walked to the door. Turning back for one last look at them, she said, "Thank you for making me feel again. Thank you for loving me, but I just don't think it's enough."

She went out the door, and briefly she wondered if the men would follow her. As she reached the tree line she took off running. Tears were streaming down her face as she flew through the brush running faster than she had ever run in her life. She could feel the branches slapping at her face, and the weeds tearing at her ankles as she ran, but she couldn't stop. She had to get away from the pain, and as far away from the twins as possible.

Just as she broke through the trees to the main cabin, she spotted Liam climbing into an old red pickup truck and he seemed to see her, and instinctively know that something was wrong. He stepped back out of the truck, and reached his arms out to catch her as she collapsed into his arms.

"Caroline? What's wrong? Are you okay?" he asked, trying to check her for injuries, and not finding any, he started to push her behind him protectively, as though someone might be chasing her.

"Please, Liam, I need to go. Please take me back to town," she pleaded with him, pulling at his arm.

"Okay, ummm… Do I need to get Dev or Damon?" The heart-broken look in her eyes told him that was not the right answer, and he held his hands up in front of him. "Okay, never mind, come on and climb in. I'll take you to town, princess." He helped her into the passenger side of the truck and then got back in himself.

As they drove down the road toward town, she asked him if she could borrow his cell phone. He gave it to her and listened quietly as she placed a call.

Caroline took a deep breath as she tried to focus her eyes on the cell phone in her hand. She wanted to go home to her apartment and be alone, but she knew there was no apartment anymore. She called the one person she knew she could. Relief coursed through her as Tina answered on the first ring.

"Caroline! I'm surprised to hear from you! I figured it would be days before those two sexy men let you out of the bed," Tina answered with a chuckle.

"Tina? Hey, I'm on my way into town, and I need a place to stay for just a bit. Can I come to your place?" Her voice quivered, and she couldn't stop it.

"What? What happened, Caroline? Where are the twins?" Tina was now alert and aware that Caroline was upset.

"I can't explain right now. Can I please just come to your place?"

"Of course, come on over. I'll get out the ice cream, and we can talk." Caroline was so relieved that she smiled at Tina's easy acceptance.

"That sounds great. I should be there in the next half an hour. I'm having a friend drop me off. See you soon." She hung up and turned to Liam.

"Thank you. I know you don't understand, but thank you for helping me," she said to him quietly.

"Well, you're welcome. I will always be there to help you if you need it. Do you want to tell me what happened?" His eyes darted between her and the road in front of him.

"No. I can't talk about it yet. It hurts too much." He nodded as if he expected that answer, and they rode in silence for a little while. She let her mind go through the last few days and feel all the pain, and all the happiness she had experienced in such a short amount of time. Liam fidgeted in the silence, and she turned her attention to him to keep herself from thinking about the twins.

"Liam, why don't you have a mate?" she asked him, breaking the tense silence, and watching him for his reaction.

He took a huge sigh, and she could see the pain and grief on his face when he started to explain. "I was married about five years ago to a woman that I met at a bar. Roxy was a sexy little number that I took home with me on the first night and married in Vegas a couple of weeks later. We found out quickly that we had mistaken lust for love, but by that point she was pregnant. Wolves are raised to honor our commitments, so I stayed. For three years I tolerated her cheating on me, and humiliating me in front of my friends and family because she had given me the greatest gift ever. My daughter, Daphne."

"That's the name on your tattoo! I wondered…" Caroline bit her tongue when she realized she had interrupted his story. With a nod of her head, she urged him to continue.

"Daphne was perfect. She was wolf, but I hadn't explained it all to Roxy. I came home after a full moon run with the pack one weekend to find my daughter in her crib wearing a dirty diaper and crying her heart out. My *wife* was passed out in the arms of another man in our bed. I took Daphne with me and filed for divorce and full custody. Unfortunately, the courts tend to favor mothers, and having no proof of Roxy's infidelity, the judge granted her residential custody. She came to pick her up, and I thought I was going to die. We argued, and Roxy tore out of the driveway with my perfect child in the back seat. That was the last time I saw her alive." Tears in his eyes, he stared out at the black night, and Caroline knew he was reliving his pain. She put her hand on his arm to comfort him. "They spun out of control on the highway, and the car rolled. Daphne was killed instantly, and Roxy died on the way to the hospital. I died that day, too."

"I'm so sorry for your pain, Liam. I can't imagine the grief you must feel for your child. I don't understand, though? I thought when wolves mated that if one mate dies the other usually dies, too," she said in confusion. He smiled grimly and gave a sharp, angry laugh.

"I never mated Roxy. I was young and didn't want to wait around hoping to stumble over my soul mate someday. Roxy never even knew I was a werewolf. I could never bring myself to share that part of me with her. It was convenient that I had to go away for twenty-four-hour shifts at the firehouse regularly. I let her believe I was at work when there was a full moon so that I could join the pack for a run. I hid the most important part of me, because I was afraid she would reject it." He sounded angry at his youthful fears, but Caroline could understand his reasons. She had hidden so much from Devin and Damon for almost the same reasons and look where it had gotten her.

"Caroline? They love you. You know that, right? They would do anything for you. Do they know where you are?"

"No, but they know I have left. And they know why. Love isn't always enough, Liam." She turned back away from him, hoping he would drop the subject.

"I don't think you should be alone."

"I won't be. Tina will be with me." Her chin jutted out, and her tone dared him to challenge her.

"Barton Diego doesn't know you have left the Gray Pack, and he is still looking for you. Please let me call the guys, or at least let me stay with you so that you are protected? You are my Alpha's mate, and I can't let anything happen to you. I've sworn to protect you," he pleaded with her.

"Thank you, but that's not necessary, Liam. I will be fine, and I want you to promise me you will not call the guys. I have left all that behind me, and chalked it up to a lapse in judgment. I'm going to get my life back on track. Tina will let me stay with her while I look for a new place, and I can go back to work. I need my normal life back." Her arms were crossed across her chest, and her body language was belligerent now. He shook his head and drove the rest of the way to town in silence.

～

As Liam pulled into the driveway of Tina's house, Caroline turned to him. He watched her cautiously, seeing the pain and sadness that swamped her.

"Can you please do me one more favor, Liam?" she whispered with her hand on the truck door handle.

"Anything for you, princess." He smiled gently at her, hoping it would relax her.

"Can you let me know occasionally that Devin and Damon are okay? I love them so much, but I can't be with them. I won't be able to contact them without it hurting, but I need to know that they are okay every now and then." She was staring off into space at some unknown spot, and Liam clenched his eyes shut.

"Oh fuck, Caroline! What have you done? Please let me call the guys," he asked as he dropped his forehead down onto his steering wheel. Devin was going to kill him, and then Damon was going to kill him again! She wasn't just running away for a little bit of space, she was running away for good.

"Please? Just do me this one favor?" she pleaded with him. "Thank you for sharing your past with me, and for being there for me when I needed help. I couldn't ask for a better friend." And then when he didn't respond, she jumped from the truck and ran inside the house.

Liam threw the truck in reverse and headed back to the den, intending on finding Devin and Damon as quickly as possible to explain. As he reached the end of the block, he slammed on the brakes.

Fuck this, he thought. *I'm not leaving her here unprotected.* He parked the truck at a convenience store about two blocks away from Tina's, and braced himself before he called Devin and Damon.

"Where is she?" Devin's voice growled into the phone.

"She's okay, Dev. What the hell did you guys do to her? She had me take her to her friend, Tina's, and she wouldn't tell me what was going on. She just said that she couldn't be what you needed, and that she needed her other life back. What's going on?" he said.

"We're on our way." Devin's words were sharp and short, and he hung up without any explanation to Liam.

Hanging up, he went back to watch the house until his Alpha could get there to collect his missing mate. He hoped that Devin wouldn't blame him for this whole thing. All he did was try to help Caroline. As he reached the spot where he and Caroline had talked in the driveway, he caught an amazing scent that sent his libido skyrocketing. He knew instinctively that this scent belonged to his mate, and his eyes darted, looking for the woman it came from. As he turned toward the small house, following the delicious smell, he got a whiff of another wolf.

Barton! The thought flashed through his brain as he connected the smell with the same one that he had found in the vandalized house yesterday. His eyes flew to the front window of Tina's house, which now had the curtains drawn. They had been open just a few moments ago when he had dropped Caroline off. His wolf rose to the challenge, and he had to concentrate to keep himself from changing and storming the house. His gut told him that Barton was in the house with

Tina, Caroline, and apparently his mate, but he also knew that he couldn't protect them and fight him without backup.

He pulled his phone out and called Devin back. He had to hold his phone away from his ear as he heard the painful howl break from Devin's throat. Then he stuck it back in his pocket to wait.

CHAPTER THIRTEEN

*C*aroline's heart was beating so fast she was afraid she would have a heart attack. Her captor was finishing tying her ankles to the dining room chair just like he had already done with her wrists. Tina sat a few feet away on the other side of the dining room table, restrained in the same fashion. Caroline's head throbbed, as she tried to remember the sequence of events prior to her waking up in this chair.

She had flown into the house blinded by tears and anxious to put more distance between her and the wolves. She had slammed through the front door calling Tina's name, and turned toward the living room expecting to find her friend waiting to comfort her. She smelled a sour smell, and then when Tina wasn't waiting for her in the living room, she realized that something was wrong. She turned toward the kitchen, but she was too late. Her attacker knocked her out with a quick hit to the back of her head, and when she came to, she was already half-bound to the chair.

"Well, well, well. You're back with us again." As the man finished tying her up, he stood up in front of her, and used his thumb and finger to roughly pull her chin upward. Her eyes met his, and she grimaced. He was a dirty-looking man who she knew was the same age as Devin, but looked to be in his late forties. He had several days' worth of beard growth on his face, and he was stocky, and soft but not really fat. He just wasn't as muscular as the men of the Gray Pack. His hair was light brown with faint gray streaks through it, and his eyes were so dark brown they were almost black. Right now they were glaring at her with anger and hatred. His clothing stunk, and Caroline knew without a doubt that this must be Barton Diego.

"He will find you, Barton, and when he does he will kill you." She said it so matter-of-factly that it seemed to catch him off guard. Then he smiled an evil grin at her, making her stomach summersault with nausea.

"So, you know who I am, huh? Good, at least you will know my name well enough to scream it when I fuck their smell off of you." He licked his thin lips and growled low in his throat as she blanched with disgust. "Nasty smell of Gray all over you. Wonder how he will feel when he finds the leftover pieces of you with my scent all over them.

She forced herself to calm her breathing and try to think clearly. She had to find a way to get her and Tina out of this mess. There was no way in hell she was going to let him rape and kill them without a hell of a fight.

Damn it, why did I leave the den? Devin and Damon told me I was in danger, and I ran away because I was scared. Why didn't I let Liam stay? Now what am I going to do? She watched him as he moved to the front window and peeked out around the curtains.

"He will be here soon," she said, keeping her voice intentionally calm, and trying to throw his confidence. She was hoping he would believe her, and run away to keep from getting caught.

"Whatever. I heard you and your human friend talking on the phone. You left him, and he doesn't know where you are yet. Even if he figures it out quickly, he will just barely arrive in time to hear your screams. Don't worry, pretty girl, I will let you watch when I kill him, or maybe I will let him watch while I kill you." He moved back to her side and gripped her hair in his hand, pulling hard to make her look at him. "Don't fuck with me, pretty girl. I wonder if I should start with your friend, that way I can show you what I have planned for you. You know what they say, anticipation always makes it better. If your boyfriend doesn't get here soon, he will miss out on all the fun!"

As he spoke, he had moved over to Tina and ran his hand over her breasts, and up the side of her face. Tina paled and shuddered. Caroline had never felt the urge to kill someone in her life until now, and watching him threaten her closest friend broke her control.

"*No*! Leave her alone, Barton," she yelled at him. "Let her go, and I will do anything you want. She doesn't know anything about this. Devin won't come for her, but he will come for me. He doesn't even know where I am right now. Let her go and find him so that he will hurry here to rescue me. Then you can finish this stupid challenge."

She could smell Tina's terror, and she desperately wished she could talk to her for a moment. She had been bound with the same rope as Caroline, but Caroline noticed that Tina's bonds were much looser. Barton must have been rushing to tie her up so that he was ready when Caroline had arrived. She wondered how he had known where to find her? She had to keep him distracted and talking to give herself time to figure out how to escape.

"You will do whatever I want anyways, so what difference does it make? This way I get a two for one deal." He was eyeballing Tina now, and that pissed Caroline off.

"I'm impressed that you were able to locate me. I didn't even know I was coming here until thirty minutes ago. How did you know where to find me?" she asked, and it caused Barton to turn and look at her cautiously.

He took a moment considering her question, and then he answered with a laugh. "It was a lucky break for me that I was able to chat with a friend of yours from the hospital. Carter was his name. He was very willing to give up your friend Tina's name so that your concerned 'uncle' could find out where you went and help you. Then it was just a matter of a quick internet search to locate her home. She and I were just going to play for a bit until she shared her knowledge of your current location, but right before I hit her I heard her on the phone telling you to come on over. Imagine my surprise that you were just going to throw yourself into my arms. It was too perfect. So here we are!" He clapped his hands together with his last statement, laughing and seeming very pleased with himself.

"You have what you wanted, Barton. You have me at your mercy. Let her go." She was determined to at least protect Tina from this deviant, whatever the cost to herself.

"Maybe. Then again, maybe not. I plan on taking my sweet time and having a good fuck either way, but first I think I will fix myself a nice meal. I haven't eaten lately as I've been searching for you, and I will need my energy to make sure I'm the last thing you remember from this life." He moved off into the kitchen, and Caroline sighed her relief.

Once he was in the kitchen banging around, Caroline took the chance to speak to Tina quietly.

"Tina, if you have a chance, you have to run. Run to the neighbors and have them call 9-1-1, and then call the firehouse. The guys there are friends of Devin and Damon's. They will be able to get me out of here. This man is an enemy of Devin's and wants to use me to hurt him. I'm so sorry you got caught up in this," Caroline whispered as loudly as she dared, and Tina nodded her understanding to Caroline and then twisted her hands in her bonds, trying hard to pull them free. Caroline watched her, praying as hard as she could that the guys would hear her frantic pleas for help and reach them in time.

"Don't worry so much about me. I'm a survivor, and this punk isn't going to get an easy ride out of me!" Tina's eyes flashed fire, and Caroline almost laughed out loud. She looked around to make sure that Barton hadn't heard them, and then started calling out to the twins in her mind.

~

Devin, help me! Damon, I'm with Barton at Tina's, please come fast. Please, guys, hear me and help me!

Devin's heart ached as he heard the pleas faintly in his mind. His mate needed him, and he was still ten minutes away from her.

We're coming, sugar.

We're on our way, Caroline!

Devin was relieved to hear Damon's voice in his mind as well. They were in separate vehicles as Devin had taken off instantly with his only goal being to reach Caroline, and Damon had backtracked a bit to gather reinforcements after Liam called to tell them Barton had her.

He pushed his truck as fast as it would go, and just prayed that no one got into his way. As he whipped the truck into a parking space next to Liam's at the convenience store, he jumped from it and took off at a run to reach Tina's house. Liam caught him just before he smashed out into the open in front of the house, and tugged him down behind a parked minivan on the street.

"Damn, that was a fast trip," Liam said, and the awe in his voice was evident.

"What's happening?" Devin growled. He could feel his claws breaking through his skin, and his body changing. He couldn't control it because he was so pissed off and scared.

"I don't know. He shut the curtains, and I'm afraid he will smell me if I get much closer. Can you tell if she is okay? What do we do?"

"Yes, she is scared, but I think she is okay for the moment. It's definitely Barton because I can smell his rank ass from here. Damon and the rest of the guys will be in here any second, and I have to get my wolf under control. Give me a minute." After a few seconds Devin realized that he was feeling his mate's fear in his mind, and it was keeping him on the brink of changing. He gave up trying to control it and let his claws extend from his skin.

"Dev, I need you to know that my mate is in there, too," Liam said with barely concealed rage.

"Huh? Your mate?" Devin couldn't hide his shock.

"I can smell her. I don't know why she would be in there, but I know she is. I don't even know who she is!" Liam cracked his knuckles in a frustrated, nervous gesture.

"Okay. We have to focus on getting the women all out safely, and then we will figure it all out. Hold it together for me, man. We can't all fall apart, those women need us." Devin's words seemed to help calm Liam some.

He sighed with a sense of relief when Damon, Cash, Owen, Rafe, and Ryley all bounded up to them. He could see the glow in Damon's eyes and knew exactly how he felt. Damon was struggling to keep his wolf under control, too. Standing there in midchange, he wanted to make a plan with the men. He had to get his mate out of there safely and end this whole thing once and for all.

"Where is she?" Damon barked.

Liam quickly explained the events of the last thirty minutes, and Damon started forward toward the house. Devin snagged his arm and met his angry gaze with a determined look. His claws were gripping Damon's wrist, and he could feel the course hair sprouting from Damon's skin as he fought the change, too.

"Damon. It's the full moon, and a brand-new wolf is in that house with a madman. She can't control her change, and the moon is rising. Once it's up Barton will be surprised to find an angry and scared young wolf on his hands. There are also humans in there that need to be protected as well. We have to have a plan or someone will get hurt." His words sounded much more calm than he actually felt, but he knew what he was saying was logical.

"Fuck, I forgot about the full moon. She can't go through this change alone. She will be scared, and stronger than even she realizes." The pain and fear for his mate was naked in Devin's eyes, and he looked back and forth between Devin and the house for a moment before he took a deep breath and hung his head. "Okay, what's the plan?"

~

Caroline could see that Barton was almost finished eating the pork chops he had found in the refrigerator, and he kept leering over at her from where he stood in the kitchen. Her stomach rolled at the thought of him touching her. She knew if he came too close to her, she would throw up, and she figured that would really piss him off. She had yet to see him with a weapon, but the baseball bat that he had used on her head earlier still leaned against the wall next to the TV. If only she could reach it in time. Tina now had one hand free, and was working at the knot on the other hand. Caroline tried not to watch her because she was afraid it would draw Barton's attention and make him look at her more closely. This was their only hope of escape.

She suddenly heard her men in her mind and felt the relief course through her body like a warm caress.

We're here, beautiful, stay calm.

Thank God! I'm so sorry that I ran away.

Sugar, tell us what's going on, but don't look him in the eyes. He is an Alpha, and he will sense that you are communicating with us.

Caroline closed her eyes and let her head fall forward so that her hair covered part of her face. If Barton watched her, she could only hope that he would think she was silently praying, because she was so overcome with fear.

Barton has us both tied to chairs in the dining room. Just inside the front door and to the left. He has been eating something to store up energy he says, before the main event. I think he's waiting for you guys, hoping you will come to find me, using me as bait. He is in the kitchen which is about fifteen feet farther to the left of us. He is closer to the side door that leads into the laundry room. Tina has one hand free from the ropes, but she can't get the knot loose on her other arm. I can't move more than a half an inch. If she can get free, I told her to run to you guys. Please make sure she gets away from him safely. I can't get out without someone releasing my ropes, and if he releases them, it will only be to kill me. He has made it clear that he intends to hurt you by raping me before he kills me. I would rather die fighting him than let him rape me.

We're coming, sugar, but you have to stay calm. Listen to me. We are going to surround the house, and then Damon and Liam are coming in the kitchen door while

I break through the front door. All of the guys are here, and he doesn't stand a chance against all of us, but to protect you guys we have to catch him off guard. We won't let him touch you, but we have to make sure we have a plan so that you won't get hurt. I want him dead at the end of this.

"What's your problem, pretty girl?" Barton's hot breath on her face caused her stomach to heave violently, and she whipped her head up to stare into his ebony eyes. "Shit, you're talking with your man, huh? So he made it here in time after all. Good, now I know he will hear it when I fuck you." With that he ripped the rope from her ankles, he moved away from her to avoid her swift kick. His eyes were full of laughter, and pure evil. He was enjoying fighting with her. It seemed to be turning him on. He roughly jerked the rope from her wrists and held them tightly in his own hands as he threw her from the chair to the floor and landed heavily on top of her.

"Come on, pretty girl, let me show you how a real wolf fucks." She gagged at his words, and had to bite her tongue to keep from vomiting.

The impact of the floor had knocked the wind out of her, and her eyesight blurred for a moment. She felt him pulling her shirt from her body and then heard her bra rip as he threw it away. His disgusting mouth latched violently onto her nipple, and he bit her hard. She screamed and fought with everything in her as he planted his knees between her thighs. He pinned her hands above her head in one hand, while his other hand pulled her jeans down her hips. He had to lift away from her to pull them down her legs, and she took the moment of imbalance to thrust her hips upward, knocking him off her to the side, and loosening his grip on her hands.

"Fuck you, asshole!" she screamed at him. She rolled quickly to her stomach and felt him heave up on top of her as if he were going to mount her from behind. The fear in her belly exploded when she felt his hard penis touch the back of one of her thighs, and then she felt the strange surge of strength race through her body.

Her bones seemed to unfold painfully as her back arched and her head snapped back. Barton fell from her heavily, and she turned to see what happened. Tina stood over him with the baseball bat, and he was clearly dazed. Caroline laughed inside when she realized that Tina had just beat him with the bat, but her attention was taken up by the pain in her muscles as she felt her body changing shape.

Barton now stared at her with wild eyes as he and Tina both watched her shift. Tina's face was a mask of shock and admiration as she took in her friend's secret. She seemed to have forgotten the bat in her hands and the devil on the floor for a moment. Caroline knew that she was changing, but having never done it before, she was terrified. Suddenly she was on four paws instead of her hands and knees, and she could feel her anger at the man in front of her gripping her wolf form. She snarled at him, and Barton smiled evilly. He quickly shifted into a huge brown-and-gray wolf. He was baring his teeth at her, and the growl that echoed through him was deep and angry.

Tina made a split-second decision when she realized that Barton wasn't going to give up on Caroline yet, and she swung her bat at his head. His strong jaws snapped the piece of wood like a matchstick, and he turned back to Caroline. Without a thought to her own safety, Tina jumped on the wolf's back, drawing his attention back to her. Caroline saw Barton's teeth graze Tina's arm as he threw the poor girl off of his back. She hit the wall with a dull thud, and she just lay there, stunned.

Caroline couldn't stop to check on her because Barton was now stalking toward her. He was the predator, and she was his prey. If she could just slow him down long enough for the guys to get inside. She howled in pain as his huge wolf form suddenly landed on her back and brought her to the floor. She felt his teeth puncture the skin on the back of her neck as he bit into her to hold her still. She fought him, twisting and turning. Shaking her wolf's body until she worked loose of him, she was able to turn her head enough to bite into his ear. She felt his rage as he smashed her face back into the floor, and then, just as she felt him trying to mount her in wolf form, Caroline heard loud crashes behind them. Several terrifying growls preceded Barton being lifted free from her prone body.

She rolled to her side and felt the blackness trying to swallow her as pain screamed through her body. Before she passed out, she saw the two huge black wolves tearing Barton into pieces, and Tina trembling in the corner of the room with tears rolling down her cheeks as Liam held her in his arms tightly. Caroline sighed with relief that they were both safe, and let the darkness consume her.

~

Caroline came back to consciousness a little while later, wrapped in a large blanket. Devin pulled her into his arms tightly and held her. "Devin?" she whimpered.

"I'm here, sugar, it's okay. He's not going to hurt you anymore. We have you." He soothed her with his hands, and kissed her head gently as she came back to reality.

"I'm so sorry I ran away from you," she cried.

"Shh…We can talk more at home. I know why you left, and I understand it. Rest now," he murmured.

"I thought he was going to kill me!" she exclaimed.

"Not a chance, darling," Damon whispered into her ear as he kissed her temple and stroked his own hands over her body, trying to soothe her.

She smiled at his words and then sighed, letting herself drift back into oblivion, wrapped tightly in his strong arms.

~

Tina watched as the man kneeling in front of her gently bandage the bite wound on her arm. He was beautiful. He had short black hair and icy-blue eyes that seemed to see more than she wanted him to. The glint of a gold ring in his eyebrow gave him a dangerous look, but his touch was so soft that she felt safe with him. His gaze seemed to burn her skin when he looked at her, and she was having trouble thinking straight. He said that he was a fellow firefighter with Caroline's boyfriends, and she couldn't shake off the memory of their first interaction by phone. He had flirted with her then, causing her to blush, and it was damned hard to make her blush.

"Thank you, Liam," she said to him. He paused, and looked up meeting her eyes.

"You're welcome. Are you in pain?" he asked. His voice was a deep baritone that rumbled through her, causing her insides to quiver.

"No. Just shaken up a bit. Not every day a girl participates in an epic wolf battle." She laughed, and stretched her back muscles, trying to ease the ache there. The heat that flared in his eyes as he watched her sinuous moves made her nipples ache. She swallowed hard and squeezed her thighs together.

"We don't usually allow humans to see us in wolf form, but I guess this falls under collateral damage," he said, shaking his head and looking back to where he was taping the gauze to her arm.

"Collateral damage? Hmm, just what every woman wants to be. Well, thanks for the Band-Aid, but I think I need to go over and check on Caroline." She pulled away from him, trying to stand. Her legs shook and her stomach tumbled. She put her hand to her forehead, trying to calm the nausea the sudden movement caused.

"Caroline is fine. She is with her mates now, and they will take very good care of her. You need to rest for a little while. Please, let me take care of you," he said, putting one hand lightly on her hip while he tipped her chin up with the other, forcing her to look at him.

"I can take care of me without help, hotshot. Thanks. I need to go back in the house and clean up the mess. There was blood and guts everywhere. I think I need to take an aspirin, too." She didn't pull away from him even though her words were dismissive. She had never felt herself respond like this to a man. Not even her now deceased fiancé had turned her on just by touching her.

"It is already taken care of. My cousins finished cleaning it up while I was checking your head and back for injuries. I don't want you to go back in there right now. You will come and stay with me tonight, that way I can take care of you. I need to watch you to make sure you don't have a concussion." His tone was determined, and she blanched.

"Huh? Wait a second. I appreciate that someone else cleaned up because I don't have a lick of energy left, but that doesn't mean I will just do whatever you want. I'm not about to sleep in a stranger's house out of some strange urge you have to take care of me. Besides, I'm a nurse so I know the signs of a concussion. If I thought I had one, I would have gone to the hospital." She crossed her arms in front of her, and leaned back to glare into his eyes. His gaze narrowed at her obvious challenge, and he growled softly. She wondered for just a moment if she should be scared of him. She had just seen him as a wolf not an hour ago, and God knows what he could do to her if she pissed him off.

"I know, but after the emotional scare you had this evening, I think it is best that you stay with someone, and the only one with the right to be that close to you is me," he said.

"You? Why do you think you have any right to be close to me?" She was stunned, and pissed. The trickle of fear in her belly was now more apprehensive and anxious than scared. This man was sexy as hell, and his dominant words were making her wet she was so horny. But she'd be damned if she would just roll over and play the easy fuck for him.

"Because you are my mate," he replied, and she felt all the blood drain from her face just before the ground came rushing toward her.

EPILOGUE

*C*aroline ran through the forest on four paws, and enjoyed the feeling of the soft grasses beneath her and the huge trees overhead. It had been a month since that terrible encounter with Barton Diego, and she was now enjoying her wolf to its fullest extent. The first time she had shifted intentionally had been about two weeks ago when she had done it out of spite because Damon was teasing her. When she had changed, she had not expected the two men to stand there staring at her completely dumbfounded, and she had quickly shifted back.

After a few tense moments they had explained with their hands and bodies how delicious her wolf form was to them, and she had since embraced her wolf. She enjoyed the feeling of freedom she had when she was in animal form, and she enjoyed the animalistic desire that came over her men when they saw her wolf.

That first couple of days after the attack, Caroline had spent in a daze, and she had pulled away from everyone around her. When she finally broke out of it, she had gone looking for her men. They were waiting for her with open arms, and they listened as she dumped all her thoughts and fears on them. They had been honest with her about wanting to marry and start a family, but they also understood that she wouldn't give up her career right now. They had soothed her fears about her debts and responsibilities, and even offered to help her pay off the bills so that she wouldn't worry anymore. They knew that she would decline their help, because she needed to prove to herself she could finish what she started. She needed to pay the bills off to complete the grieving process.

After a fantastic weekend of reunion sex, the men had proposed to her again, but in a more traditional way this time. It had been decided that she would marry Devin legally, because he was the oldest and the Alpha, but she knew that she was actually marrying them both in her heart. In her public life, she would present Devin as her husband, and Damon as her brother-in-law. In their private life and in their pack life, she would honor them both as her husbands. She now wore a stunning engagement ring made out of two bands that were braided together, one silver and one gold. The delicate bands met in the middle, and were held together by a large white diamond. They explained that they chose it as a symbol of the two of them held together by her, their mate, their sole reason for existence. She cherished the ring, and looked forward to presenting them with rings of their own on their wedding day. The wedding was being planned, and she had already asked Tina to be her maid of honor.

She laughed to herself when she thought about the wedding. She had wanted to go ahead and just elope, but Devin and Damon wanted a large wedding in front of the whole pack. They said that they wanted to show her off, and make a statement of their joint commitment to her. They had even pushed her into planning a shopping trip next weekend for a wedding dress. It was a sweet gesture, but she hoped they would understand her new need to speed plans up.

She had gone back to her job at the hospital after her vacation time was up, and she and the guys had decided to continue living in town, and just visiting the den when their shifts at the firehouse allowed. The night of the fight, they had all been stunned to find out that Tina was Liam's mate. Caroline laughed as she remembered the look of shock and pure desire that had turned her friend's face white and then bright pink when Liam had announced that Tina was his mate, and would be going home with him instead of staying in the home where she was attacked. He was already very protective of his mate, just like the twins were of Caroline. She wondered how long it would take him to gain Tina's trust. Tina carried a lot of baggage from her past, and had created a lot of defensive walls around her heart. She also wondered if Liam had shared his own personal tragedy with Tina yet. She knew that Tina was pushing him away, but she could see the sparks between them when they were together, so she had hope for them. They had a long road to walk, but they would find their way to each other, just like Caroline found her home with Devin and Damon.

As she ran through the trees, she heard the pounding of paws behind her, and she slowed a bit. She wanted them to reach her, and quickly. Her men caught up to her, and she came to a stop whipping around to greet them. Devin shifted first and slowly stalked toward her, completely nude. Damon followed suit a moment later.

They were grinning like Cheshire cats, and she knew that her quick call via telepathy had ripped them from whatever tasks they were doing a few moments ago. They certainly hadn't hesitated to come find her!

"Hey there, beautiful, did you need us?" Damon asked her as he placed a hand on her jaw and she kissed his palm. He couldn't restrain the passion in his voice as he stared into her eyes. She nodded, and opened her arms to him. He took her mouth, sucking the air from her lungs, until she felt like he was breathing for her. She could feel Devin's hands gripping her hips as he came to stand behind her, and his mouth kissed along her shoulder up her neck to her ear.

"Good. Show us," Devin rumbled right into her ear, and her knees buckled. She slid to the ground between them, and ran her hands across their naked cocks. She loved the feeling of velvet over iron strength, and she let herself tease them. Licking first one and then the other, she watched them enjoy her touch with pure and passionate abandon. Her thighs grew damp with her juices, and she felt her own clit throb as she tasted them.

Devin broke first and grabbed her hair in his fist, directing her to swallow his cock deeper into her throat. She groaned at the dominance in his gesture and purposely tugged her head a bit to get him to grip her hair tighter, and push her farther. Behind her she felt Damon on his knees, pressed against her naked ass. His fingers slid through her wet lips, and he stroked her from clit to ass and back, repaying her teasing in kind. She shuddered when he finally pushed his finger into her tight rosebud, and thrust his cock hard into her pussy. His head hit her cervix before he reared back and shoved forward again, forcing her farther down Devin's hot length.

"Suck me, sugar. Take me deep." Devin's voice had deepened with his passion, and she could hear Damon growling behind her as he fucked her harder. Her spine arched in a show of submission to them, and she gagged slightly on Devin's cock as she climaxed. Wave after wave of fire rippled through her body, and Devin let her pull away from him. She heard herself growl when Damon pulled away from her, too, leaving her empty and alone.

"Hold on, beautiful, we aren't done yet. Come here and ride me." Damon had dropped to the soft grass beside her and was spread out waiting for her. She threw her leg over his hips and used her hand to guide him until he was lined up. She sank down slowly, relishing the electric shocks that went through her at the contact. She felt a hand on the back of her neck, pushing her forward over Damon until her breasts were smashed to his chest and her ass swayed open in the air. Using her own juices, Devin's fingers slipped easily into her ass, and she could feel the two of them move gently in a rhythm, bringing her back to the edge of an orgasm.

It hit her, and she screamed when Devin's teeth sunk into her shoulder to hold her steady as his cock replaced his fingers. Pushing past the tight ring of muscles, he sunk all the way into her. Her feeling of fullness was completely overwhelming, and she whimpered.

"Please. Please…" she moaned into Damon's chest.

"Fuck, you're tight," was all Devin could grind out, and he started to pull back gently. The two men set an easy pattern together, and took Caroline on a violent roller coaster of orgasms. She couldn't imagine how they were holding back their own climaxes when they kept driving her body farther and farther.

Damon released his seed into her womb first and dug his fingers deep into her hips. The feeling of him spurting into her hot passage drove her over the last peak, and she felt darkness swallow her as she felt Devin's release into her ass. She let herself collapse onto Damon again, completely sated.

When she woke a couple of hours later, her men still held her tightly. Her head was pillowed on Damon's stomach, and her legs draped over Devin's lap. She caught Devin's eyes and held his gaze. He grinned at her easy blush and chuckled.

"After all that passion, you can still blush? Damn. I love you, sugar." His voice was wrought with emotion, and Caroline's eyes filled with unshed tears.

"I love you, too." She slowly lifted off of the men, and stood, brushing grass and dirt from her back. Taking a deep breath, she spoke, "I need to tell you something…"

Both men were on their feet in a second, and Devin lifted her chin until he could look deep in her eyes. Concern etched his features. "What's wrong, sugar?"

"Nothing. Everything is perfect." She paused and lifted her mouth to his with a gentle kiss. Then she turned to kiss Damon as well. When they both looked slightly scared, she giggled, and pulled their hands to her belly. "Remember how you talked about wanting to have a family…"

"Oh my God! You're pregnant? Really!" Damon yelled at the top of his lungs, hugging her from the side when she nodded. Devin laughed out loud, and pulling her from Damon, he spun her around. She couldn't hold her own peel of laughter as she felt her feet return to the grass.

"Damn, sugar! That's the sexiest thing I've ever heard. I can't wait to see you swollen with our pup." His mouth met hers, and she could taste the love on him. While Devin kissed her mouth, Damon knelt in front of her, kissing her naked stomach.

"I guess we will have to move the wedding up just a little bit?" she whispered into Devin's mouth.

"Done. Just so long as you're the bride, and I'm one of your grooms, I don't care when we get married." Damon spoke against her belly, and they all laughed together.

Knowing that their child rested deep within her made her love for them swell to the surface, and she let it soar free as the two men surrounded her. As they made love again in the grass and shadows of the forest she thanked God for bringing her back to life, and now allowing her to create life. In eight months or so, she would have a completed family again, and she couldn't wait.

THE END

WWW.LORIKINGBOOKS.COM

ABOUT THE AUTHOR

Lori King is the author of more than thirty Amazon best-selling romance novels, as well as a full-time wife and mother of three boys. Although she rarely has time to just enjoy feminine pursuits; at heart she is a hopeless romantic. She spends her days dreaming up Alpha men, and her nights telling their stories. An admitted TV and book junkie, she can be found relaxing with a steamy story, or binging in an entire season of some show online. She gives her parents all the credit for her unique sense of humor and acceptance of all forms of love. There are no two loves alike, but you can love more than one with your whole heart.

With the motto: Live, Laugh, and Love like today is your only chance, she will continue to write as long as you continue to read. Thank you for taking the time to indulge in a good Happily Ever After with her. Find out more about her current projects at http://lorikingbooks.com.

EXCERPT FROM REFLECTIONS OF THE WOLF

The Gray Pack 2

Reflections of the Wolf

After being rescued from a crazy werewolf with murderous intent, Tina Jameson has a scorching night with Liam Gray, local firefighter and Beta Wolf of the Gray Pack. When he announces that she is predestined to be his mate, she is fast to push him away.

Suddenly she finds herself in a whirlwind of conflicting emotions and rioting desires. Having been a victim of a senseless act of violence in her past, Tina has given up on a forever kind of love, even if that man turns her on like no one else has.

Liam didn't think he wanted a mate, but his wolf wants Tina in his bed and his life for good. In order to have her he must let go of the guilt he has from his daughter's death and then help Tina to let go of her own tragic past. Can one night determine their destiny, or will fear drive them apart?

Prologue:

The First Impression

Ring… Ring… Ring…

"Battalion One, Liam Gray here."

"Hello, umm…is this the fire station on Rock Road?"

"Sure is, honey. Do you have a fire you need put out?"

"Is Damon Gray there?"

"Who's calling?"

"It's personal. Is Damon there?"

"That depends on who's calling. You sound too sweet for Damon's tastes. How'd he manage to find you?"

"He didn't find me. He found my friend, and then he met me. Are you going to help me or not?"

"A friend or a *friend*, doll? Because there's a hell of a difference."

"Are you fucking kidding me? Look, hotshot, I'm a friend of Caroline Trainor's, and since he left the hospital with her, I'm hoping he knows how I can get ahold of her. Now stopping fucking around and put him on the damn phone."

"Holy hell, girl, you've got a mouth on you. Your voice is too sexy to use words like that."

"Lord have mercy. Never mind, just put your supervisor on the phone."

"Now, hold on a minute. I didn't say I wouldn't help you. But before I ask a girl out, I need to know how much competition I have."

"Ask me out? Is this really the fire station? Are you insane?"

"I've been called crazy before, but definitely not insane. This is the fire station, and Damon isn't on shift tonight, but I will pass on your message to him…if you agree to go out with me."

"I am not going out with a complete stranger. I'm not stupid."

"Hey, I introduced myself already, so if anyone would be dating a stranger it would be me. What's your name, sweetheart?"

"Listen, Caroline is my best friend, and I let her walk out of the hospital with Damon and his brother, because she trusted them. I should have known better than to trust men that look that good. If he turns out to be some sort of freak…"

"Trust me, Damon and Devin Gray are the least freaky of this bunch, and not even the best looking. Now, if you won't tell me your name, how am I supposed to tell him who to call?"

"It's Tina Jameson. I work with Caroline at the hospital, and I really need to talk to her. Do you have a phone number for him?"

"Tina, yeah, that suits your voice. I like Tina. Let me make you a deal, Sweet Tina. I will pass the message on to Damon later today if you will meet me for drinks tomorrow night."

"Ugh! This is ridiculous. I am not going out for drinks with you, Liam. I just need you to give him the message."

"I like hearing you say my name, Sweet Tina. I will give him the message, and maybe soon you and I can have that drink."

"Don't hold your breath."

The phone disconnected, and Liam hung his end up with a smile on his face. Well, that was fun, he thought to himself. I definitely have to meet this woman. Chuckling to himself, he pulled his personal cell phone from his pocket and started dialing Damon Gray's number.

Purchase Reflections of the Wolf at www. LoriKingBooks.com

ALSO BY LORI KING

Fantasy Surrender

The Gray Pack Series

Paranormal Suspense

Fire of the Wolf

Reflections of the Wolf

Legacy of the Wolf

Dreams of the Wolf

Caress of the Wolf

Honor of the Wolf

Apache Crossing

Sidney's Triple Shot

Sunset Point

Point of Seduction

Storm Corps

The Marine's Seduction

Pieced Together

Tempting Tanner

www.LoriKingBooks.com

Made in United States
Orlando, FL
21 February 2024

43950166R00114